Dolly Alderton Biography

Everything I Know About Love A Memoir, Friends, Job, Life, Paties, Dates

This Book is for:

....

....

....

....

....

Copyright © 2023 by ASHLEY ROLANDE BYERS
All rights reserved.

The content of this book may not be reproduced, duplicated, or transmitted without the author's or publisher's express written permission. Under no circumstances will the publisher or author be held liable or legally responsible for any damages, reparation, or monetary loss caused by the information contained in this book, whether directly or indirectly.

Legal Notice:
This publication is copyrighted. It is strictly for personal use only. You may not change, distribute, sell, use, quote, or paraphrase any part of this book without the author's or publisher's permission.

Disclaimer Notice:
Please keep in mind that the information in this document is only for educational and entertainment purposes. Every effort has been made to present accurate, up-to-date, reliable, and comprehensive information. There are no express or implied warranties. Readers understand that the author is not providing legal, financial, medical, or professional advice. This book's content was compiled from a variety of sources. Please seek the advice of a licensed professional before attempting any of the techniques described in this book. By reading this document, the reader agrees that the author is not liable for any direct or indirect losses incurred as a result of using the information contained within this document, including, but not limited to, errors, omissions, or inaccuracies.

CONTENTS

CHAPTER 1
Everything I Knew as a Teenager About Love

CHAPTER 2
Boys

CHAPTER 3
The Bad Date Diaries: Twelve Minutes

CHAPTER 4
Four servings of Hangover Mac and Cheese

CHAPTER 5
The Bad Date Diaries: A Hotel on a Main Road in Ealing

CHAPTER 6
Being a Little Overweight, Being a Little Underweight

CHAPTER 7
Everything I Knew About Love when I Was 21

CHAPTER 8
What I Am Afraid Of

CHAPTER 9
The Most Annoying Statements Made by Humans
CHAPTER 10
The Unexciting Women of Unexciting Camden

CHAPTER 11
The Seducer's Sole Meunière Recipe

CHAPTER 12
Apple pizza topped with Can't be Arsed ice cream

CHAPTER 13
The Bad Date Diaries: A Restaurant Bill for £300

CHAPTER 14
The Bad Party Chronicles: Christmas 2014 at My House in
Camden

CHAPTER 15
Expelled from the Club Sandwich Recipe

CHAPTER 16
The Bad Date Diaries: A Mid-morning, Completely Sober
Snog

CHAPTER 17
Everything I Knew About Love when I Was 25

CHAPTER 18
Why You Should Have a Boyfriend and Why You Should
Not Have a Boyfriend
CHAPTER 19
Weekly Grocery List

CHAPTER 20
Recipe: Scrambled Eggs

CHAPTER 21
My Therapist Tells Me

CHAPTER 22
Heartache Hotel

CHAPTER 23
I Got Gurued

CHAPTER 24
Enough

CHAPTER 25
Twenty-eight years of learning twenty of lessons

CHAPTER 26
Return home

CHAPTER 27
Everything I Know at Age 28 About Love

CHAPTER 1
Everything I Knew as a Teenager About Love

Romantic love is the most significant and fascinating phenomenon in the entire universe.

If you don't have it when you're a mature adult, you've failed, just like so many of my art instructors, who I've noticed have frizzy hair and ethnic jewelry.

It is essential to have a lot of sex with a large number of individuals, but no more than ten.

When I am a single woman in London, I will be exceedingly elegant and slim, wearing black dresses and drinking Martinis, and I will only meet men at book launches and gallery openings.

True love is demonstrated when two guys fight physically over you. The sweet spot is when blood is extracted without anyone having to go to the hospital. Hopefully, this will occur to me one day.

It is essential to lose your virginity between the ages of seventeen and eighteen. Literally, even the day before is acceptable; however, if you enter your eighteenth year as a virgin, you will never have intercourse.

It's fine to kiss as many people as you want; it doesn't signify anything, it's just practice.

The most popular males are always tall, Jewish, and possess a car.

Boys of adolescent age are the most desirable because they are more sophisticated, cosmopolitan, and have looser standards.
When companions have partners, they become monotonous. An acquaintance having a boyfriend is only amusing if you also have one.

If you never ask your friend about their boyfriend, they will eventually realize that you find it tedious and cease talking about him.

After you've lived a bit, it's a good idea to get married. Say thirty-sless.

Farly and I will never have the same crush because she prefers boys who are short and cocky, such as Nigel Harman, whereas I prefer men who are macho and enigmatic, such as Charlie Simpson from Busted. Because of this, our friendship will endure forever.

There will never be a more humiliating moment in my life than when I attempted to kiss Sam Leeman and he pulled away and I collapsed to the ground.

Boys enjoy it when you are impolite to them, whereas they find it childish and uncool if you are too sweet.

When I ultimately have a boyfriend, everything else will be irrelevant.

CHAPTER 2
Boys

For some, the ecstatic shrieks of their siblings playing in the garden were the defining sound of their youth. For others, it was the chain rattling of their much-loved bike, hobbling along hills and vales. Some will recall hearing birdsong as they walked to school, or the laughter and kicking of footballs in the courtyard. It was the sound of AOL dial-up internet for me. I am still able to recall it note for note. The tiny initial phone noises, the reedy, half-completed sound squiggles that indicated a half-connection, the high one note that indicated progress was being made, followed by two abrasive low thumps, and white fuzz. The subsequent silence indicated that the worst of the situation had passed. A soothing voice said, "Welcome to AOL," with an upward inflection on the letter 'O'. Followed by the phrase, 'You have email.' I would prance around the room to the dial-up sound of AOL to pass the agonizing time more quickly. I composed a dance routine using ballet moves: plié on the alarms and pas de chat on the thumps. I did it daily after returning home from school. Because that was my life's soundtrack. Due to the fact that I spent my youth on the internet.

Growing up in Stanmore, one is neither urban nor pastoral. I was too far away from London to be one of those cool kids who went to the Ministry of Sound, dropped their 'g's, and wore vintage clothing purchased from surprisingly excellent Oxfam stores in Peckham Rye. But I was too far from the Chilterns to be one of those ruddy-cheeked, feral, country adolescents who wore old fisherman's sweaters, learned to drive their father's Citron at the age of thirteen, went on nature walks with their cousins, and smoked acid in a forest. This was especially true if you were an adolescent dependent on your mother's availability to transport you in her Volkswagen Golf GTI. My best companion, Farly, was only 3.5 miles away by bicycle from my cul-de-sac. He was and remains unlike any other individual in my life. When we were 11 years old, we met at school. She was and continues to be my polar antithesis. She is darker than I am. She is slightly too diminutive, whereas I am slightly too tall. She plans and organizes everything, whereas I wait until the last minute. She enjoys order, whereas I tend toward disorder.

Morrissey once described his adolescence as 'waiting for a bus that never arrived'; this feeling is exacerbated when coming of age in a place that resembles a beige waiting room. I was tired, depressed, and lonely, restlessly wishing away the hours of my youth. Then, like a valiant knight in dazzling armor, AOL dial-up internet appeared on the large desktop computer of my family. Then MSN Instant Messenger appeared. When I downloaded MSN Messenger and began adding email address acquaintances – friends from school, friends of friends, and friends from nearby schools that I had never met – it felt like tapping on a prison cell wall and hearing a response. It was like discovering vegetation on Mars. It was similar to turning on the radio and hearing the crackling transform into a human voice. It was a retreat from my suburban monotony into a plethora of human life.

MSN was more than a method I kept in touch with my friends as a teenager; it was a place. As I recall it, it was a room in which I physically sat for hours and hours every evening and weekend, until my eyes became bloodshot from gazing at the screen. The rest of my family was basking in the Provencal sunlight by the pool while reading, but my parents knew there was no point in arguing with me about MSN Messenger. It was the epicenter of my alliances. It was my personal sanctuary. It was the only possession I could claim as my own. As stated, it was a location. But MSN brought the email addresses and avatars of these new floating Phantom Boys; they were generously donated by females at my school who hung out with boys on weekends and then generously distributed their email addresses to the student body. Every female at my school added them as a contact, and we each had our fifteen minutes of fame conversing with them.

I hastily compiled a Rolodex of these orphans and strays, assigning them a designation in my contact list labeled 'BOYS'. We'd spend weeks discussing GCSE options, our favorite bands, how much we smoked and drank, and 'how far' we'd 'been' with the opposite sex (always a momentarily labored work of fiction). The introduction of virtual males into the lives of our schoolmates introduced an entirely new set of conflicts and drama. Who was speaking to whom would be the subject of constant rumor milling. Girls would pledge their faith to boys they had never met by inserting the boy's first name with stars, hearts, and underscores on either side into their username. MSN had a complicated protocol; if you and a boy you liked were both logged on, but he wasn't talking to you, a surefire way to get his attention was to log off and then log back on; he would be notified of your return and hopefully initiate a conversation.

Lauren, a girl with untamed hair, freckles, and hazel eyes with kohl-rimmed rims, became my best friend when I was fifteen. Our relationship was more intense than anything that had ever transpired in the MSN Instant Messenger windows. Since we were children, we had seen each other at random Hollywood Bowl birthday parties, but we eventually met through our mutual friend Jess over dinner at one of Stanmore's many Italian chain restaurants. The relationship reminded me of every ITV2 romantic movie I've ever seen. We talked until our mouths were dry, we finish each other's sentences, we made tables turn round as we laughed like drains; Jess went home and we sat on a bench in the freezing cold after we got chucked out of the restaurant just so we could continue on talking.

She was a guitarist seeking a singer to form a band; I had performed at a sparsely attended open-mic night in Hoxton and was searching for a guitarist. The next day, we began rehearsing bossa nova renditions of Dead Kennedys songs in her mother's shed, with 'Raging Pankhurst' as our working band name. We later altered it to the even more inexplicable 'Sophie Can't Fly'. Our first performance was in a Turkish restaurant in Pinner, with only one patron who was neither a family member nor a school friend. A theater foyer in Rickmansworth, a pub garden's derelict outbuilding in Mill Hill, and a cricket pavilion just outside of Cheltenham were subsequent projects. We performed on any thoroughfare without a police officer. We sang at any bar mitzvah reception that would have us. We envisioned ourselves as a two-person Bloomsbury Group of early 2000s MSN Messenger. But just as I became friends with Lauren, I fled the suburbs to attend a coed boarding school seventy-five miles north of Stanmore. MSN could no longer serve my fascination around the opposite sex; I needed to know what they were like in real life.

As it turned out, I discovered that I had essentially nothing in common with the majority of boys and little interest in them, unless I could kiss them. And no male I wanted to kiss wanted to kiss me, so I might as well have stayed in Stanmore and continued to enjoy a series of fantasy relationships in the fertile landscapes of my imagination. I attribute my high expectations for love to two factors: first, being the offspring of parents who are almost embarrassingly infatuated with each other, and second, the films I viewed as a child. I had an unusual obsession with old musicals as a child, and having grown up utterly addicted to the films of Gene Kelly and Rock Hudson, I had always expected males to carry themselves with the same elegance and charm. However, the introduction of coeducation quickly disproved this notion. Farly visited me on the weekends and gawked at the hundreds of boys of all shapes and sizes carrying sports backpacks and hockey sticks over their shoulders as they wandered the streets. She could not believe my good fortune that I was able to sit in chapel pews near them every morning. By the time I graduated from high school, I no longer used MSN Messenger as frequently as I once did. The beginning of my first semester at Exeter University coincided with the introduction of Facebook. Facebook was an online treasure trove for males, and this time it was even better because you had all their vital information on one page. If MSN was a blank canvas on which I could paint my wildest fantasies, Facebook messaging was a solely functional tool for arranging meetings. It was how students determined their next target; how they scheduled their next Thursday evening.

By the time I graduated from college and moved back to London, I had given up the practice of cold-calling potential love prospects on Facebook with the aggressiveness of an Avon salesperson, but a new pattern was emerging. I would meet a man through a friend, at a party, or on a night out, obtain his contact information, and then develop an epistolary relationship with him via text or email for weeks and weeks before confirming a second in-person meeting. Perhaps it was because this was the only way I had learned to get to know someone, with a distance between us and enough space for me to curate and filter the best possible version of myself – all the good jokes, the best sentences, and the songs I knew he'd enjoy, which were typically sent to me by Lauren. Any woman who spent her formative years surrounded only by other girls will tell you the same thing: you never truly shake the notion that males are the most fascinating, alluring, repulsive, and bizarre creatures to roam the earth; as dangerous and mythical as a Sasquatch. Typically, it also indicates that you are a verified fantasist for life. It is remarkable how accustomed you become to the intense intensity of fantasy when you frequently escape into it. I always believed that my fascination and obsession with the opposite sex would subside once I entered adulthood, but I was just as ignorant about how to interact with them in my late twenties as I was when I first opened MSN Messenger. Boys posed a difficulty. One whose repair would take me fifteen years.

CHAPTER 3
The Bad Date Diaries: Twelve Minutes

It is the year 2002. I am 14 years of age. I'm wearing a kilt skirt from Miss Selfridge, a pair of black Dr. Martens, and a bright orange crop top. The youngster is Betzalel, a school acquaintance of Natalie, a friend of mine. They met at a Jewish summer camp and have been exchanging relationship and life advice over MSN ever since. Natalie is in search of new friends, having recently lost hers by spreading a false rumor that a girl in our class self-harms when, in reality, she just has terrible eczema, and I am one of her targets.She suggests that she set Betz and I up on MSN Messenger since she knows I want a partner. Natalie provides me with a new boy to converse with, and in exchange, I occasionally have lunch with her. I am more than satisfied with this unspoken arrangement. After a month of speaking every day after school on MSN, Betz and I are essentially dating. I share his view that everyone his age is infantile, and he is also tall for his age, as am I. We frequently discuss these shared experiences. We agreed to meet at Costa in the Brent Cross retail mall. I invite Farley so that I am not alone. Betz arrives and he appears nothing like the photo he sent me; since camp, he has shaved off all of his curly hair and gained a ton of weight. We exchange greetings across the table. Betz places no orders. I inform him that we must depart because we must catch the 142 back to Stanmore. The date is twelve minutes in length. When I get home and connect on MSN, Betz immediately sends me a lengthy message that I know he has already composed on Microsoft Word and copied and pasted into the chat window using his signature purple Comic Sans italic font. Betz forbids me for a month, but he forgives me in the end. We never meet again, but we remain relationship confidants until I reach the age of seventeen. Freed from my contractual obligation, Natalie and I no longer share lunch.

CHAPTER 4
Four servings of Hangover Mac and Cheese.

For the entire immersive experience, consume this while wearing pajamas and watching Maid in Manhattan or a documentary on serial killers.
– 350g of macaroni or penne pasta is appropriate 35 grams of fat
– 35 g of common flour – 500 milliliters of whole milk
200 grams of shredded Cheddar cheese 100 grams of shredded Red Leicester cheese 100 grams of shredded Parmesan cheese 1 tablespoon of English mustard — A number of minced green onions - A dash of Worcestershire seasoning – 1 small package of shredded mozzarella cheese. — Pepper and salt for seasoning – Olive oil to Public display. Cook the pasta for eight minutes in a large pot of simmering water until it is slightly underdone; it will complete cooking in the oven. Drain and set aside the pasta, then add olive oil to prevent adhering. In a separate, large saucepan, thaw the butter. Stir in the flour and continue heating, stirring constantly for a few minutes, until a roux paste develops. Slowly blend in the milk while simmering for ten to fifteen minutes over low heat. Stir the sauce continuously as it cooks until it becomes smooth, glossy, and gradually denser. Remove the sauce from the heat and stir in the remaining Cheddar, Red Leicester, and Parmesan along with the mustard, a sprinkle of salt and pepper, the chopped onions, and a dash of Worcestershire sauce until melted. The grill should be heated to its utmost temperature. In a baking dish, pour the pasta and sauce mixture, stir in the mozzarella, and then top with the remaining Cheddar, Red Leicester, and Parmesan cheeses. The mixture should be grilled (or baked at 200°C for fifteen minutes) until the surface is golden brown and bubbling.

CHAPTER 5
The Bad Date Diaries: A Hotel on a Main Road in Ealing

It is my first Christmas after graduating from college, and I have a full-time sales position at L.K. Bennett on Bond Street. Debbie, the dazzling fashion student with the highest commission, paints my lips. Vivien Leigh reddened in the dressing room before an important engagement. Graysen is his name, and I met him at York University a month ago while visiting a high school acquaintance. I was waiting to purchase two vodka Diet Cokes at the student union bar when someone seized my hand. Graysen, with his lanky, pallid, intriguing, eyeliner-smudged Elvis eyes, flipped my palm over. "Three youngsters. You will pass away at age ninety. He regarded me. He murmured, "You've been here before," in a dramatic manner. He is the first person of my age I have ever encountered who chooses not to use Facebook. I believe him to be Sartre. He takes me to a Martini bar because he remembers I said it was my favorite drink (at this point, I am still in the "training myself to like Martinis" phase, so I worry he'll see my first-sip grimace, but I manage to conceal it). The group then proceeds to the oldest tavern in London, where I consume strawberry beer. He presents me with a set of hotel room keys; his employer has provided him with a hotel room for the night. He never indicates why.

In the time it takes him to explain to me why "London has been more of a parent to me than my parents," we've taken three buses and arrived at a drab Ealing hotel in a converted suburban home. I don't want to sleep with him because I want to get to know him better, so we spend the entire night lying in bed, gazing at the off-white ceiling, and talking about the past eighteen years of our lives. He is the son of a very ancient, very elegant, very wealthy man who was 'the last of the colonizers' and discovered a rare species of fish while traveling, wrote a book about it, and has lived off the money ever since. I am filled with awe. We fell unconscious at 5 o'clock. The following morning, Graysen must report to work at an early hour. He kisses me, bids farewell, and leaves a peach confection at my bedside. That is the final time we will ever see one another. I will spend the next five years pondering if Graysen was merely an actor seeking a gullible audience and an escape from himself for one night. If everything was fabricated: the palm reading, the hotel, the fish, and the eyeliner. Then, many years later, I will fall in love with a biology PhD student who will become my life's greatest love. On a Sunday evening, I will be lying on his bed in his sweater while he reads us a book about a man who discovered a fish. I will take it from him and examine the inside cover to find a picture of a man with the same visage and last name as Graysen. My companion will inquire as to why I'm laughing. Because everything was genuine, I will say. "And it was so absurd."

CHAPTER 6
Being a Little Overweight, Being a Little Underweight

I was only twenty-one and a month out of college. And my first legitimate beau had just broken up with me over the phone. Harry and I had been together for just over a year despite being thoroughly and completely mismatched. He was conservative, sport-obsessed, did a hundred press-ups every night before bed, was the social secretary of the Exeter University Lacrosse Club, and possessed a non-ironic 'Lash Gordon' T-shirt. He despised excessive displays of emotion, towering women in heels, and excessive volume. Essentially, the entirety of my psyche at the time. He believed I was a catastrophe, while I believed he was a square.

When we boarded a train to Oxford for Lacey's twenty-first birthday party, it was one of our lowest points during that long, hot, agitated August when we had no separation from one another. After the main course, I wandered away from my table and stumbled upon a swimming pool that looked enticing. I stripped naked and went swimming, and when a few friends came searching for me, I encouraged everyone else to do the same. The night descended into a mass pool party and I became a type of naked, poolside Master of Ceremonies. Harry got insane. The following morning, Farly and AJ hid behind a tree with uncontrollable giggles as they watched him yell "YOU WILL NEVER SHOW ME UP LIKE THAT AGAIN!" to me, my head-hanging shame was made more apparent by the fact that the pool had been over chlorinated and my bleached hair had turned a vivid bottle green.

Farly spent the night in my bed. And the following night. She stayed for two weeks; I did not return to the apartment. It was the first time I had ever experienced sorrow, and I never imagined that the overwhelming emotion would be such acute confusion; it was as if I had no reason to ever trust anyone again. I was uncertain as to what had occurred and why. I only knew that I had not been adequate. I cooked for myself during my teenage years, and I cooked for everyone during my time at university. When I was six years old, my first entry in a diary was an enthusiastic account of what I had consumed that day. I recalled periods of my life based on the food on my plate: the crispy baked potatoes of my seaside vacations in Devon, the lurid, glutinous jam tarts of my tenth birthday, and the roast chicken of every Sunday night, which coated my dread of the upcoming school week in gravy. No matter how terrible life became or how excruciating the pain, I was always confident that there would be a place for seconds. I never felt overweight, but my body type was often muddily described as 'a big lady'. I descend from a lengthy line of tall giants. My brother, God bless him, was a seven-foot-tall adolescent who had to browse for clothes in stores with names like "Magnus" and "High and Mighty." When I was fourteen, I was five feet ten inches tall.

As a teen, I struggled with my height – I never knew how much I was supposed to weigh, because every female was half my height and referred to their 'fat weight' as a weight I hadn't been since childhood, which instilled a profound sense of shame. I was browsing for size 16 garments before I was sixteen. When I attended boarding school, I gradually lost weight, and by the time I entered university, I was a comfortable size 14 – but I didn't object that I wasn't particularly slim. I continued to kiss the males I desired. I am able to wear Topshop. And I enjoyed cuisine and cooking immensely. I understood that to be the trade-off involved. Nevertheless, here I was. Finally unable to consume any food. My entire body was flooded with a sickly yellow sensation, and my appetite, my most valuable asset, has vanished. My intestinal tract felt active. I constantly had a lump in my esophagus. Mum would give me bowls of soup in the evening, claiming it was simple to swallow, but I would only eat a few spoonfuls before pouring the rest down the drain.

After two weeks, I stepped on the scales. I was missing a stone. I saw, for the first time in my life, the beginnings of what I had been led to believe were the genuine characteristics of femininity as I stood naked in front of the mirror. The waist, pelvic bones, collarbones, and shoulder blades are reduced in size. In this new, incomprehensible environment – where the boy I'd shared a home and life with for over a year was abruptly repulsed by me – I felt a flicker of understanding. I had ceased eating, so my body began to change. It succeeded. Here, in the chaos, I discovered a simple formula that I mastered. Here was something I could influence that would take me somewhere new, where I could be someone different. The answer was found in my reflection: cease eating. I made a project out of my new objective; I weighed myself every day, counted my steps and calories, did sit-ups every morning and night in my bedroom, and recorded my weekly measurements. I subsisted solely on Diet Coke and carrot spears. If I were hungry, I would go to bed or take a steamy bath. Even more weight was lost. I lost it daily, pound by pound, and it never appeared to plateau.

By the end of December, I had lost three stones. Three months to lose three pounds. It became more difficult for me to summon the thoughts and rituals that had kept me from eating up until that point. I was fatigued, my hair was thinning, and I was bone-chillingly cold at all times. I attempted to warm up in the shower with the water so hot that it burned my back and left traces. I continually lied to my anxious parents about how much I had eaten that day and when I would eat next. I would awaken in tears of frustration because I had foolishly broken the spell I had cast by dreaming that I had ingested mountains upon mountains of food. Hicks remained at Exeter for an additional year following our graduation. Sophie, Farly, and I decided to travel down to spend a weekend with her and visit our old haunts. It also meant I would be able to see Harry, who was in his final year at the school, which I hoped would give me a sense of completion. I informed him that we needed to return each other's belongings, and he agreed to meet with me.

I engaged in weight loss with greater intensity and haste. My rage gave me energy. I began to reach a weight plateau, a sign that the mechanisms of my metabolism were misaligned and slowing down, so I ate even less. Friends began confronting me about it, and Farley told me she believed I was obsessed. She attempted to assist me in opening up, but I dismissed her inquiries with humor. I realized that an effective way to get people off my back was to constantly make jokes about the small amount of food I was consuming. I would bring it up before anyone else, so they would know that it was not a problem, but merely a diet. Moreover, I kept pointing out that I was still a size 10. I was not underweight; I was initially overweight. I continued because it was the only factor I could influence. I persisted because I simply desired happiness, and it is common knowledge that being thinner makes one joyful. I persisted because society rewarded me at every turn for my self-inflicted torment. I received compliments, received propositions, felt more accepted by strangers, and nearly every piece of clothing looked fantastic on me.

The problem is that a woman can never really be slender enough. Being constantly hungry, restricting an entire food group, or spending four nights a week in a Fitness First facility are not considered to be excessive costs. To be empirically attractive as a young male, all you need is a nice smile, an average body type (give or take a stone), some hair, and a decent sweater. To be a desirable woman, there are no limitations. Have all of your body's surfaces groomed. Perform manicures weekly. Everyday, wear heels. Even if you work in an office, dress like a Victoria's Secret Angel. It is not sufficient to be an average-sized woman with some hair and an acceptable sweater. That is insufficient. We are instructed to resemble the women who are compensated for their appearance. When I first met Leo, I was meandering around a filthy house party in Elephant and Castle. I had never seen a more flawless man before. He was tall and slender with dark, unkempt hair, a strong jaw, sparkling eyes, a retroussé nose, and a seventies mustache. His face was a cross between Josh Brolin and James Taylor, and the best part was that he had no notion of his own beauty. He was a bohemian PhD candidate with a monomaniacal monobrow.

At the conclusion of one of our nights together, he would walk me to the bus stop outside Chalk Farm station, where I would wait for the N5 to transport me ten miles north to Edgware. From there, I would take a 45-minute walk westward to Stanmore, meandering through deserted streets lined with Volkswagens and red-brick semi-detached homes, and I was happier than I ever imagined I could be. Leo hadn't realized my secret, because I didn't want him to think I was a nutcase, but after a few months of dating, he tallied a few things up. I was able to avoid all situations involving food; I always told him that I would consume breakfast after we parted in the morning. A friend informed him that she believed I was unwell. I would have done anything to maintain his presence in my existence. The love I felt for him was aggressive and tense; I loved him with dread and ardor. I was not the one to fall in love; rather, I was the recipient. As if a ton of bricks were dropped from a tremendous height. I had no choice but to abandon an obsession that was threatening to destroy everything.

Thus I did. I read the appropriate literature and visited the doctor. Slowly, a stone returned to me. I gradually adapted to eating ordinarily. My health improved. I even tried group support meetings in community centers where, would you believe, the first thing they do is put a plate of biscuits in the middle of the room and fuss over whose turn it is on the rota to bring the snacks the following week, which seemed to me to be as useful as putting a bottle of Jack Daniel's in the middle of an AA meeting. I fell in love with cooking again. I fell in love with dining again. I spent every weekend with Leo doing both. My mother and I viewed old episodes of Fanny Cradock and Nigella together. Everyone kept telling me I looked 'healthy' whenever they saw me, and I attempted to ignore the thought that this meant I was once again overweight. The conflict ended, and recovery commenced. I was given my existence back. The weight I regained was not something I chose to do on my own volition. I believe I would have continued to lose weight if I hadn't met Leo, but he helped me achieve a complete recovery. As I grew older and thankfully became more cognizant of what a priceless gift a healthy, functioning body is, I felt humiliated and perplexed that I had treated mine so poorly. You cannot forget your precise weight each week and month during that time period. No matter how hard you try to ignore it, there are days when you feel like you'll never feel as ebullient as the 10-year-old girl who was licking lurid jam off her fingertips.

CHAPTER 7
Everything I Knew About Love when I Was 21

Men adore untamed, unclean women. Have sex on the first date, keep them up all night, smoke hash in their bed in the morning, never call them back, tell them you despise them, show up at their doorstep dressed as an Ann Summers nurse, and be anything but conventional. This is how you maintain their interest. Never again will a breakup be as difficult as the initial one. You'll float around aimlessly in the months afterwards, feeling as lost and bewildered as a child, questioning all the things you knew to be true and contemplating all the things you have to relearn. Always stay at a man's home, and then you can depart in the morning whenever you please. The ideal male has olive skin, brown or green eyes, a large, strong nose, a thick beard, and dark, curly hair. He has non-embarrassing tattoos and five pairs of vintage Levis. When you are not having intercourse, you should have a bush similar to a wild, climbing shrub. There is no purpose in wasting time, money, and fumes on hair-removal cream if no one will see the results. When you reach a healthy weight, you will be content with who you are, and you will be worthy of affection. Do not date a person who will not allow you to get inebriated and flirt with other people. If this is a part of your identity, they should accept you as you are.

Orgasms are simple to simulate and are beneficial for both parties.

Perform a kind act today.

When you fall in love with the perfect man, you'll feel settled, centered, and peaceful.

The worst sensation in the universe is being rejected.

In general, men are not trustworthy.

The initial three months of a relationship are the most enjoyable.

A true friend will always prioritize you over a man.

When you can't fall asleep, fantasize about all of your future relationships with olive-skinned, curly-haired males.

CHAPTER 8
What I Am Afraid Of

– Death

– People I adore passing away

– Drunk men on the street telling me I'm tall, fat, sexy, ugly, and ugly – Drunk men on the street telling me to cheer up – Drunk men on the street telling me they want to shag me – Drunk people 'trying on' (stealing) my clothes – Drunk people 'trying on' (stealing) my clothes – Drunk people 'trying on' (stealing) m&ms – Drunk people 'try

– Falling out of a window – Accidental infanticide – Parlour sports

– Discussing American political history – Starting fires. Not comprehending the washing machine everywhere – The Cancer

– Sexually Transmitted Diseases – Wooden Lollipop Sticks – Plane Crashes

– Plane food

– Occupying an office

– Being asked why I believe in the above – Being asked if I believe in God (a little) – Being asked if I believe in horoscopes (a little) Incurring an unplanned overdraft – Never having had a dog

CHAPTER 9
The Most Annoying Statements Made by Humans

– 'I'm not having an appetizer, are you?'
– 'I'm more of a guys' girl'
– 'I'm a natural salesperson' – 'I'm in a relationship!'
– 'You're always late' – 'You were quite inebriated last night'
– 'You've told me this story before' – 'He says it like it is'
— 'She's very beautiful'
– "I believe you require a glass of water"
– 'I'm quite OCD'
– "Our relationship is extremely complicated"
– 'Would you like to sign Alison's greeting card?'
– "Let's go as a group"
– "Let's get caught up!"
– "Have you encountered this?"
Marilyn Monroe wore a size 16 dress.
– "Your next dental appointment is due."
– 'When was the last time you backed up?'
How do you find the opportunity to tweet so frequently?
— 'Sorry, it's been crazy'
The term 'Holibobs'

CHAPTER 10
The Unexciting Women of Unexciting Camden

At the age of twenty-four, during my first year residing in London with Fairly and AJ, I met a friend for a drink on a Tuesday evening after work. Despite my efforts to keep her out until closing time, she had to leave the bar at half past eight due to an early morning appointment. I texted everyone in my phonebook who I thought might be available and interested in spending the night with me, but everyone was occupied or in bed. I felt restless and disappointed that I couldn't stay out for just one more hour and one more glass of wine, so I sulkily boarded the 24 bus – my trusty conveyance that carried me from the center of London to my doorstep in twenty minutes – and rode home. It is a feeling I grew very accustomed to – panicked and throaty; a sense that everyone in London was having a good time except for me; that there were pots of experiential gold hidden around every street corner and I wasn't finding them; that one day I would die, so why bring any potentially perfect and glorious day to a premature end by going to bed early?

The arrival of the 24 at the pub at the end of my street roused me from my gloom. It was a NW5 slum, a once-famous music venue turned squalid watering hole for Camden's early risers. I exited the carriage and entered. It was my first visit since the day we moved in, when we were informed that Farly had made history by being the first customer to order coffee in forty years. The landlord went across the road to the corner shop to purchase some Nescafé Gold Blend and milk and charged her 26p. I ordered a beer and made small talk with the bartender, who seemed entirely oblivious to the fact that he was serving yet another lone patron. A man in his late sixties with a gray yeti beard inquired about my day, and I lamented the absence of a drinking companion to accompany me throughout the evening. He claimed he was the ideal candidate for the position. I left at midnight, scribbling the man's phone number on the back of a beer mat with the mutual agreement that we'd spend an afternoon together listening to records, but knowing I'd never contact him again. He was merely "a night," of which I wished for many. A memory, an experience, an anecdote, and a new visage. The following evening, when I returned home from work with an immovable hangover to find Farly and AJ snoozing on the couch, I told them how I had ended up in a dingy tavern down the street the night before.

I am so thankful that, as an adolescent, I fetishized the coffee-spoon-sized details of adulthood so vividly, because the relief of finally reaching adulthood has meant that I have found very little of it to be a burden. It has been a joy to pay my own rent. I have enjoyed preparing for myself daily. Even sitting in the GP's waiting room gave me pleasure, knowing I had registered and gotten myself there without assistance. I have never, ever gotten over the fact that I no longer have to consume gin from shampoo bottles, that there are no lights-out, and that I can stay up watching movies or writing on weeknights until four in the morning if I so choose. I am relieved, energized, and revitalized to be able to consume breakfast foods for dinner, play records extremely loudly, and smoke outside my window. I still can't comprehend my good fortune. My entire existence as a young adult in my twenties resembled that of Macaulay Culkin in Home Alone 2: Lost in New York, when he checks into The Plaza, orders mountains of ice cream from room service, and watches gangster films. I solely attribute this to a disciplined upbringing.

We spent three months searching for our first adult residence in London. Our budget was limited, and it was difficult to locate apartments with three double bedrooms. AJ remarked, "All we'd do here is stay in and watch The X Factor while eating Sainsbury's Basics penne" in reference to a house in Finsbury Park that had been photographed to look like a Notting Hill mews house but, upon arrival, appeared to be a wing of Pentonville Prison. There was the disastrous viewing of the Brixton estate flat that Fairly and AJ attended with a large group of millennial aspirants queuing outside like they were at Madame Tussauds. The real estate agent neglected to bring the keys, so he kept everyone waiting for half an hour. After a three-minute tour of the dump, they were forced to lie on the ground because a gunman was being pursued by police outside the property. Just as we were about to give up, Farley discovered a three-bedroom apartment within our price range through a private landlord on Gumtree.

It was near a notoriously dangerous crescent that connected the Chalk Farm end of Camden Town to the Kentish Town end. It had a twice-weekly traditional market that sold five-pound slippers and cartoon bed sheets, a daily fruit and vegetable vendor, and a cash-only independent supermarket that sold marijuana from under the sandwich counter. It was ostentatious and extravagantly beautiful. The home was a magnificent wreck. One of a row of 1970s ex-council maisonettes made of Lego-yellow blocks with odd placement and proportions of windows and doors, as if constructed in a hurry by a teenager playing The Sims. The front garden had two overgrown bushes that meant, in the summer, you couldn't make your way through the decaying wooden front gate without vigorous arm-swiping. The tiling in the kitchen was decorated with images of the English countryside. The backyard was overgrown with vegetation. There were strange liquid streak markings on the hallway wall, which, after extensive investigation, we could only conclude were urine. Everything smelled very wet. Above us, intruders occupied the apartment. Gordon, the proprietor, was a handsome man in his forties with a boxy leather jacket and suspiciously dark, frizzy hair. He wanted everyone to know that he was a BBC news presenter: his voice was loud and posh, and his manner was absurdly abrupt and informal.

It was crooked, wobbly, and eccentric, but we knew it was the ideal first home for our extended family and friends, whom we intended to invite over every weekend. We returned downstairs to inform Gordon of our request; he was in the midst of a phone call. To cover our deposits, we scrimped and saved, so the first month was spent in thrilling, frantic, frenetic frugality. Farley purchased a bundle of Post-its to label various surfaces with messages such as 'TV WILL BE HERE' and 'TOASTER WILL BE HERE' because we had almost nothing for the house. We had Marmite and cucumber sandwiches for dinner every night. The second night in our new home, I returned to find both girls wearing wellies in the living room because they had spotted a mouse and didn't want it to run over their bare feet as they attempted to capture it. Farly purchased a block of Pilgrims Choice Cheddar from the Nisa Local, placed it in an empty vanity case, and dragged it across the carpet in an attempt to lure the rodent to safety.

We also became acquainted with the proprietor of the local corner store, a middle-aged man with the physique of a marine named Ivan. On our first visit, he ominously told us that if we 'fell into any difficulty with any gangs' to come to him immediately as it would be 'dealt with'. At the time, Farly was donning a string of pearls. However, I felt oddly secure knowing that Ivan was never more than ten seconds away from our front door, and that he always came to the rescue whenever the rodent issue recurred. Frequently, I would dash out of the house barefoot and in pajamas and into the store yelling, "IT'S BACK, IVAN! "IT'S BACK!" was exclaimed with Blanche DuBois-like hysteria. Camden seemed like the ideal location for us: it was central, close to all the finest parks, and, best of all, dangerously, hopelessly uncool. No one of our age lived there, nor did any of our acquaintances. When we went out on Camden High Street, we encountered hordes of Spanish teenagers on a school excursion and men in their forties with Paul Weller haircuts and winkle-picker shoes who were still waiting for Camden's Britpop glory days to return.

Occasionally during the years we lived in East London, we would attend a party or a night out and be surrounded by young, beautiful, and hip people, and we would question if this was where we were supposed to be at our age. As we departed, however, we were always exhausted by the experience and thankful that we lived in a place where we never had to appear to be cooler than we actually were, which was not very often. We could go shopping in leggings, sweatshirts, and no bra without running into anyone we knew. We could easily dominate a dance floor by performing a drunken, comedic cancan in a line and still be the trendiest people in the entire bar. We could go out and devote the entire evening to each other, without attempting to impress anyone else. Simply put, there was no one left in Camden to impress.

One of the first items I purchased for the house was a soup kitchen-sized industrial cooking pot. Our friends have always been excellent eaters, so I was delighted to have my own stove and kitchen table. In our first years of living together, we hosted supper parties three times per week. I calculated the most cost-effective meals to prepare: pot after pot of dhal and tray after tray of Parmigiana. In the summer, we would have candlelit dinners in our hideously overgrown garden; at one point, it was so overgrown that a tree caught fire in a bizarrely biblical manner, and we all poured saucepans of water and glasses of Ivan's subpar five-pound Sauvignon Blanc on it while inebriated. In my first couple of years residing in London, I eliminated the majority of drug experimentation from my system. First, I established a familial rapport with Fergus, a genial drug dealer. Fergus was not a dealer who would sit in the car and pass you a baggie under the dashboard; rather, he would join me late on a Friday night when I had friends over for dinner, rolling spliffs at the table and telling long-winded jokes while eating the leftovers, until I finally sent him packing with a Tupperware container of spaghetti carbonara.

Farly, who had always been more sensible than I was and was always in bed by midnight when we had guests over for dinner, never had the pleasure of meeting Fergus, but was always perplexed by the way I referred to him as a "cousin or family friend." She was awakened at 4:00 a.m. one night by the sound of me giving Fergus a strolling tour of the house while he advised me on the feng shui of each room. The following morning, she entered my room to find me huffing and wheezing as I moved my bed to the opposite wall. Fergus dropped out of contact rather abruptly, as I was told they often do, so I was then pointed in the direction of CJ – who was a steadfast disaster. CJ was renowned as London's worst narcotic dealer. His punctuality was appalling; he would routinely give the 'wrong order' to the 'wrong customer' and then request the 'product' back half an hour later. His phone never received a charge. His sat nav constantly malfunctioned. At one point, after he had kept me waiting for an hour and a half, I told him on the phone that he was "his own worst enemy" in an exasperated teacher-like manner. On the Thursday before I left London for a music festival, I called him and asked if he could sell me some MDMA.

Regardless of how I obtained them or from whom, the acquisition of drugs was almost always more thrilling than the drugs themselves. Talking about whether to get some, dialing the number, and getting the cash out; someone waiting in the apartment while another person went to find the car, and returning with a tiny plastic bag containing herbs or powder; and the promise of what was to come – that was the part that got my pulse beating the fastest. She could not believe how tediously time-consuming it was to purchase, divide, and use cocaine; she compared it to preparing shepherd's pie. But for someone who never wants a night to end, the tedious process of lining up powder and rolling spliffs is a source of pleasure – it's a diversion and an assured night extension. Go to bed at eleven o'clock, we've exhausted all possible topics of conversation, and there is an artificial desire for the party to continue indefinitely. Cocaine was only ever a means for me to continue drinking and remain awake long after I was exhausted; I was never particularly fond of the sensations it provided.

I believed that in order to be a writer, I needed to amass experiences. And I believed that every worthwhile experience and person existed only after dusk. I always remembered something Hicks said to me as we lay in bed beneath the shimmering fairy lights of her student room's window. Even when we met for a quick pad thai on a Thursday night, my companions anticipated that a night with me would ruin them for the following day. My energy, bank account, and mental state were unable to keep up. And I didn't want to self-mythologize and elevate myself into a tragic Village Drunk figure that everyone would dread scheduling coffee with, knowing that it would most likely end the following morning in a 24-hour casino in Leicester Square.

The chasm between who you were on a Saturday night, when you commandeered an entire pub garden by yelling about how you've always felt you had at least three prime-time sitcom scripts in you, and who you are on a Sunday afternoon, when you're contemplating death and wondering if the postman likes you, becomes too vast. Age brings about self-awareness. And self-awareness kills a self-proclaimed party lady instantly. I also had two completely separate careers, working in television and as a freelance writer. They demanded more and more of my time and attention, and regular binge drinking and hangovers were detrimental to my productivity and creativity. When I was on the verge of exhaustion, a friend told me, "You're attempting to lead two lives." You must choose between being the woman who works harder than everyone else or the woman who parties harder than anyone else.

I chose to pursue the latter option. Life was more abundant during the day, and there was less need to flee at night. However, it would take me some time to realize that the path to adventure does not consist solely of late evenings, hot bars, cold wine, strangers' apartments, lighted parked cars, and small amounts of powder. Throughout my twenties, I realized that alcohol had the same capacity to inhibit experience as it did to amplify it, despite the fact that I had always viewed it as a means to experience. Years later, I realized that if you continually behave in a manner that makes you feel ashamed, you will not be able to consider yourself seriously, and your self-esteem will continue to decline. Ironically, my teenage endeavor to become an adult by drinking excessively left me feeling more like a child than any other of my actions.

Throughout my twenties, I felt like I was about to be accused of something terrible, as if someone could very easily march up to me and say, "YOU'RE the dick who drank bath oil in a pint glass at my house party on a dare – you owe me £42! "; or "HEY! THROW POT!" Tuesday nights, from now until the day I expire, I will always prefer to be in a dingy Camden pub drinking beer while conversing with a total stranger. I eventually grew out of those regular blackout benders that washed out the following day like a tsunami, just as I eventually grew out of the crumbling yellow-brick mansion. Nevertheless, for a brief moment, as I sat in my overgrown garden of Eden, drinking sour Sauvignon with the women I adored, with the record player turned up loud and the empty plates piled in the sink, I believed I lived in the greatest house ever. I continue to believe that I did.

CHAPTER 11
The Seducer's Sole Meunière Recipe

(feeds two) I created this for the aforementioned musician I dated at age 24 in an attempt to win his affection. It lasted approximately one week. Since then, I've made it for other lads deserving of my time and brown butter, and the results have been more effective and long-lasting.

– 4 tablespoons of ordinary flour – 2 lemon sole filets – 1 tablespoon of rapeseed oil (or sunflower oil) – 50 grams of butter

– 2 tablespoons of cooked brown prawns - juice from half a lemon

– 1 teaspoon tarragon

– A fistful of coarsely chopped flat-leaf parsley – To season with salt and pepper Mix the flour and seasoning on a plate, then coat the filets evenly with the mixture. Get rid of excess.

Bring the oil to a high temperature. Each side of the filets must be cooked for two minutes. They should be golden and firm.

Cover the fish with foil to keep it toasty.

Reduce the pan's heat, add the butter, and melt it until it is golden brown. Remove the pan from the heat and combine the shrimp with the butter and lemon juice.

Place the sole on the platters, pour the mixture of butter and lemon over each filet, and garnish with capers and parsley. The season.

Do not serve with your large open spirit.

CHAPTER 12
Apple pizza topped with Can't be Arsed ice cream.

(four servings) A recipe given to me by my mother in order to impress guests when they arrived at my shithole for shithole dinner parties, requiring no skill or effort.

Four very fresh egg yolks are required for the ice cream. – 100g confectioners' sugar – 340g mascarpone cream – vanilla extract

Stir together egg yolks and sugar until pale and creamy.

Beat in mascarpone cheese and vanilla flavoring. Place within a Tupperware canister.

Freeze overnight or for 3–4 hours minimum.

For the apple pizza: – Pack of puff pastry – Pack of marzipan – 500g apples, peeled and cut – Jar of apricot jam

The pastry is rolled out.

Cover the cake with a marzipan ring.

On top, arrange the apple slices.

In the meantime, simmer the apricot preserves on the stovetop to a golden hue.

When the apple pizza comes out of the oven, pour the heated apricot jam on top and allow it to rest.

Serve with the frozen yogurt.

CHAPTER 13
The Bad Date Diaries: A Restaurant Bill for £300

I am on my third date with an attractive entrepreneur I met on Tinder in December 2013. He is the first wealthy man I've ever dated, and I have mixed feelings about him spending money on me. Occasionally, when he graciously pays the bill, I feel flattered, as if this is how adult courtship is supposed to operate. At other times, I feel irritated with myself for becoming so predictably emotional when an elderly man with a fast car and an alcohol problem buys me champagne. This manifests as uncontrollable rage towards him.

You cannot possess me! Three bottles of wine to the good, I yell without reason in the Mayfair restaurant he has chosen. "I'm not a thing for you to possess; I won't dress up just so you'll buy me lobster!" I can purchase it myself!

Fine, honey, purchase it for yourself, he slurs.

"I will" I screech. And not going Dutch – the ENTIRE thing

The waitress brings the bill of £300 to the table.

I use the restroom to text my roommate AJ, requesting that she lend me £200 and deposit it into my account promptly.

CHAPTER 14
The Bad Party Chronicles: Christmas 2014 at My House in Camden

Since we moved into our Camden home two and a half years ago, I have been pressing for a Rod Stewart-themed party. Rod Stewart, in my opinion, bridges the distance between the extreme campiness of Christmas and the carefree joy of a twentysomething house party. My roommates, Belle and AJ, reluctantly concur that our Christmas party should have a Rod Stewart theme, but emphasize that they do not want any responsibility for it. I prematurely age and bankrupt myself in preparation for the celebration by collecting Rod Stewart memorabilia. We have plastic cups with his face on, Rod Stewart ashtrays, mince pies customized with sugar paper Rod Stewart faces, a life-size Rod Stewart cardboard cut-out, a Rod Stewart sign signaling where the toilet is and a Rod Stewart banner with MERRY CHRISTMAS, BABY!! on it. Sabrina, India, Farly, Lauren, and Lacey arrive early to help decorate the home for Rod, and they all concur with Belle and AJ that it was a complete waste of money.

Oh God, I exclaim as I pin the banner to the wall while Sabrina holds my chair. The Faces posters I ordered have not arrived on time. Do you believe anyone will object? "No," she exhales. Nobody else will care about any of this except you. The first guests to arrive at precisely seven o'clock are my charming, somewhat boisterous, new American acquaintance whom I have only met once before and her facial-haired boyfriend. There is no doubt that they have been imbibing all day. In addition, they brought their Cavalier King Charles spaniel, who was wearing a miniature Christmas sweater. The other guests don't arrive until nine o'clock, so we attempt to catch up with our first two guests, but unfortunately, the boyfriend passes out on the couch with his spaniel on top of him for the remainder of the evening, so he is in plain view of anyone who enters the party. Friends arrive gradually, one by one. Things are awkward. The man remains unconscious with the dog on him, creating an arresting sight upon entering the party. One guest, a friend of a friend and a music video director from the cool Peckham crowd, walks in, takes one look at the scene, and departs, claiming that he forgot about another event. I go to the restroom to take a break from the crowd, which is composed of entirely dissimilar social groups with nothing to say to one another, while 'You Wear It Well' plays on repeat in the background and people complain about the Rod-only playlist. AJ and Belle are seated in the bathroom, AJ on the toilet and Belle on the edge of the Jacuzzi. We discuss how terrible the party is. We consider methods to get people to leave and end the situation. AJ states that she requires a 10-minute nap because she is exhausted and miserable. There is a knock on the bathroom door and my sibling comes in.

The celebration ends soon before midnight.
The next morning over coffee, Belle and I conduct a two-person Chilcot Inquiry into what went so horribly wrong. I suggest that my preparation for the topic may have created unrealistic expectations.
"You created a rod for your own back," she says with a wise nod.
We keep the cardboard cutout of Rod Stewart in the living room for some time. A reminder to never become arrogant in this existence. We accessorize him seasonally, donning a pink bra during the Lord Sewel hooker scandal and a leprechaun cap on Saint Patrick's Day. When we move flat eight months later and pack up the house, we leave nothing except the Rod Stewart cut-out in the center of the living room, passing the curse of bad parties on to the future tenants.

CHAPTER 15
Expelled from the Club Sandwich Recipe

(feeds two) Regularly consumed with AJ while sitting on the kitchen counter, swinging our legs and yelling about that jerk bouncer who told us we were too inebriated to re-enter the club and that we were 'letting the rest of the group down'.

– 2 eggs

– 4 slices of bread (preferably sourdough, but white Hovis will suffice) Optional: – Mayonnaise – Dijon mustard – Rocket

– Butter and olive oil for searing — Salt and pepper for seasoning Fry eggs in olive oil and a touch of butter in a pan that is extremely heated. Once or twice, drizzle the oil over the eggs to brown the yolk.

Broil the bread.

Spread one slice with mayonnaise and one slice with mustard on each sandwich.

Add one fried egg and a fistful of rocket to each sandwich. Salt and pepper are used as seasonings.

Take approximately five large, sloppy nibbles. Spread mustard on the face.

Pour any remaining alcohol into two clean containers (for us, this was typically the old bottle of Toffee Vodka Farly received for Christmas 2009 that resided in the back of the freezer).

Play a record by Marvin Gaye.

CHAPTER 16
The Bad Date Diaries: A Mid-morning, Completely Sober Snog

Springtime in 2014. I am awakened by my alarm at nine o'clock on a Saturday morning after five hours of slumber. There is a WhatsApp message from dishy American Martin: 'Doll face – we still on for a cup of joe?' My head feels like a soiled sock has been turned inside out, but I assure him I'll be there. We matched on Tinder three days ago, and since then it's been a steady stream of 'No way that's my favorite Springsteen album! ', 'I believe in reincarnation too', 'Yes, perhaps we are all wanderers', etc. As I search my room for last night's false eyelashes and re-glue them, I am convinced that he will be my boyfriend by the end of the week, and that I will move to Seattle with him the following month. For this is the only logical solution in the mind of a single, hungover woman who is humiliated because she tumbled off a bus the night before – marriage and emigration.

The ensemble consists of a massive Aran sweater that is so oversized that it hangs like a dress, denim hot pants because all of my trousers are dirty, a pair of laddered tights, and white plimsolls.

"No coat?" AJ, my hungover roommate, croaks as I pass her on the stairs.

I respond, "No need," with a carefree air.

She exclaims as I close the door, "By the way, you REEK of Baileys!"

Martin occupies a bar stool at Caravan King's Cross. Thankfully, he matches his photographs. As I arrive, he is writing in a notebook, which I believe adds a nice theatrical touch to the nomadic lost-soul agenda he promotes on his whimsical Instagram account, which I have already stalked.

What are you writing? I inquire behind his back. He turns, grins, and peers at me.

He responds, "None of your business," and then kisses me on both cheeks. We haven't even had a cup of coffee, let alone six brews, and it's already quite flirtatious. I believe this is because he is an American.

Martin relates his life tale to me. A forty-year-old illustrator from Seattle decided to use the money he earned from a lucrative position to travel the world for a year and write a book. He is engaging in Tinder tourism in order to meet new individuals. He has been in England for a month and plans to spend a few more weeks in London before continuing his travels.

After our coffees, we sit on a bench outside the café, staring at the water fountains spouting in a rhythmic, pornographic manner, and he quotes Hemingway, which I believe is excessive, but I am enjoying the imaginative tone of the date, so I go along with it. He pulls out another journal that he has illustrated with maps of every country he has visited so far, along with footprints depicting his travels. I inquire whether he has a woman in each port. He chuckles and utters "something to that effect" in his irritating, marvelous accent. He conducts me down the steps in front of Central Saint Martins art college to the canal by the hand. We walk until we are standing beneath the closest bridge, at which point he unbuttons his coat, pulls me into it, and drapes it around me. He kisses my lips, my temples, my cheeks, and my neck. We kissed for thirty minutes. The current time is 11 a.m. Martin and I separate ways at 11:30 and express gratitude for the pleasant morning. I return to bed by 12:30 and sleep the entire afternoon. I awake at four in the morning convinced that the entire event was a hallucination. Predictably, Martin disappears after our coffee morning, and when he does contact me, he is evasive about when our next date will be. A week later, after imbibing Prosecco on a Friday night and being encouraged by my friends, I sent Martin a WhatsApp message riddled with misspellings asking if I May be candid' and suggesting we begin a 'platonic but sexual relationship' while he is in London. I propose that I become his "London port girl." I inform him that it is "what Hemingway would do." I never hear from Martin again.

CHAPTER 17
Everything I Knew About Love when I Was 25

Men admire women who are reserved. Make them delay five or three dates before engaging in sexual activity. This is how you maintain their interest.

Infuriatingly, the boyfriends of your best friends will stay around. The majority of them will not be who you envisioned your best friend would wind up with.

On eBay, suspenders and stockings can be purchased cheaply and in quantity.
Online dating is for misfits, and I am included in that category. Be extremely suspicious of individuals who pay for a humiliating online dating profile.

Forget what I previously said about using hair-removal treatment when dating. If you lose your hair, you are a disgrace to the sisterhood. We must adopt an active stance against patriarchal control of the female anatomy.

Never make an album as excellent as Blood on the Tracks "our album" with a boyfriend, because you won't be able to listen to it years after you break up. Don't make that error at the age of twenty-one.

A man is not a man if he adores you because you are thin.

If you believe you want to break up with someone, but practical matters are getting in the way, this is the test: imagine you could go into a room and press a big red button that would end your relationship with no fuss. No breakup conversations, no weeping, and no returning his belongings. Would you perform the action? If the answer is yes, you must end the relationship.

If a male is 45 years old and has never been married, there is a reason. Do not linger to discover what it is.

The worst sensation in the world is when someone dumps you because they no longer fancy you.

Always bring a man back to your home, so you can convince him to remain for breakfast and manipulate him into falling in love with you.
Casual sexual encounters are rarely satisfying.

Fake orgasms will make you feel awful and guilty, and they are unfair to the man. Employ them sparingly.

Some women are fortunate, while others are not. There are both virtuous and bad people. It is a matter of pure chance who you end up with and how you are treated.

Your closest companions will leave you for males. It will be a long and drawn-out farewell, but accept it and make new acquaintances.
On lonely, sleepless nights when your anxieties crawl over your brain like cockroaches and you can't fall asleep, fantasize about a time when you were loved – in a past life of toil and blood. Remember how it felt to seek refuge in another's arms. Expect that you will locate it again.

CHAPTER 18
Why You Should Have a Boyfriend and Why You Should Not Have a Boyfriend

Motives for having a partner – Greater likelihood of receiving a decent birthday cake – Access to Sky TV? Sunday afternoons – Something to speak about – Something to talk at

– More compassion when you commit a grave error on the job – Someone to grope your derriere in line for popcorn - Holidays for one are extremely costly - And you cannot apply sunscreen to your own back – Occasionally, you cannot consume an entire large pizza by yourself - Possibly has a vehicle

– It's nice to make a sandwich for someone other than oneself. – It's nice to think about someone other than oneself. – It's nice to have regular, non-weird intercourse.

– Cozier bed

– All others have one

If you have one, people will consider you endearing; if you don't, they will consider you shallow and dysfunctional. – The relief of not being required to engage with others – The dread of dying alone, void, etc. Arguments against having a lover - Everyone except you disturbs you.

– 'Debates'

– They probably won't like Morrissey – They undoubtedly won't like Joni Mitchell – They may or may not like Bob Dylan. They will point out when you embellish your accounts. – Attending the dull birthday celebrations of their friends in Finsbury Park – Being informed of what you did while intoxicated the night before – Sharing dessert

– Being required to view any live or televised athletics – Being forced to spend time with their peers' girlfriends and discuss The Voice

– Constantly walking around between apartments with your underwear in a sack.

– Being truthful about your emotions – Having to keep your room immaculate – Not reading as much
– Constantly needing to keep your phone charged so he knows you're alive – You will likely miss interacting with others. – All over the washroom are hairs.

CHAPTER 19
Weekly Grocery List

– Toilet paper – New underwear – Paper – The desire to peruse all of the newspaper – Coffee capsules – Marmite

– Apples – Sanitary products not perfumed with Britney Spears' fragrance – Time-management skills – Pup (miniature dachshund) – Faucet dispensing strong but mild Yorkshire tea – Toaster with a more dependable timer – Flatmates who are willing to watch Countryfile with me – My very own chauffeur – Bin liners – Puppy (soft-coated Norfolk Terrier) – Jarvis Cocker – An endless supply of Cheddar – Bin liners The opportunity to view each Seinfeld episode three times – my personal cinema – Improved grammar – Greater ability to say 'no' to items – Thicker skin Twenty pairs of stockings without staircases – Milk

CHAPTER 20
Recipe: Scrambled Eggs

You only require butter, eggs, and bread. Not necessary for scrambled eggs are milk or cream. They are straightforward to prepare and eat when you're feeling down.

– 2 knobs of salted butter – 4 fresh eggs (plus one yolk if you're feeling indulgent), gently beaten with a fork — Salt and pepper for seasoning Slowly melt one knob of butter over low heat in a large saucepan.

Pour the eggs into the pan.

Move them around with a wooden spoon in a methodical and consistent manner.

Remove the pan from the heat when it is barely too moist.

Season and incorporate the remaining tablespoon of butter.

CHAPTER 21
My Therapist Tells Me

Why are you present?
How did I get there? I never expected to be there. Behind Oxford Circus, in a tiny room with cream carpets and a burgundy sofa. Where it always smelled of molecule perfume and nothing else, regardless of how deeply I sniffed upon entering – no leftover lunch, no cooling coffee – no indication of a life outside this room other than this woman's perfume. Whenever I caught a whiff of it on a woman at a party, my heart would always plummet and I would be reminded of 1 p.m. on a Friday afternoon. I was there for a price per unit of time. A commentator's box, a television studio for post-match analysis, existed in a void of life where only conversation between two individuals existed. The less popular discussion program that runs concurrently with the main event. This was the case Absolutely: It Requires Two. This was Defrosting Dancing on Ice. This was the room I always pictured when I was on the precipice of making a poor choice: in the restroom of a bar, with a man in the taxi. This room promised to alter the course of my life.

I have always vowed that I would never be in a room like this. But I had no idea where else I could have been. I had exhausted all other options. At the age of twenty-seven, I felt like I was being blown over by anxiety. Since becoming a freelancer nine months prior, I had spent virtually every day alone with my thoughts. I had disregarded the concerns of my friends and family; I was always on the precipice of tears, but unable to communicate with anyone. Every morning I awoke with no idea where I was or what was happening; I awoke to my life every morning as if the previous night's sleep had been a bloodied blow to the head. I was there because it was required of me. I was there because I had delayed going; because I always claimed I lacked money or time; and because it was self-indulgent and frivolous. I told an acquaintance that I was on the verge of imploding, and she gave me the number of a woman to contact. I was out of justifications.

I responded, "I think I'm going to fall and die." Eleanor peered over her glasses and then returned to her page, writing feverishly. She had a dark, seventies-style semi-parted fringe, feline brown eyes, and a prominent nose. She likely was in her early forties. She resembled a youthful Lauren Hutton. I observed that her arms were muscular, tanned, and graceful. I believed she probably thought I was a childish infant. A large, obese failure. A girl with excessive privilege who frittered away all her hard-earned currency so she could boast about herself for one hour per week. She likely spotted women like me from a mile away. "I can't open or close any of the windows in my apartment; I have to ask someone else to do it," I continued, holding back tears that felt like they were pressing up against the back wall of my irises like water against a flood wall. Sometimes I cannot enter a room with an open window because I am terrified of tumbling out. When a train emerges from a tunnel and draws into a tube station, I must stand with my back against the wall. I envision myself collapsing before it and dying. I observe its occurrence every time I blink. Then I'll spend all night replaying it in my mind, and I won't be able to sleep.'

She responded with an Australian dialect, "Right." "How long have you felt this way?" I stated, "Everything has deteriorated significantly over the past six months." But intermittently for the better part of ten years. When I am very apprehensive, I drink excessively. Identical to the death preoccupation. The fixation on the flavor of the month is declining. I led her through The Greatest Hits of My Ongoing Emotional Turmoil. I discussed my weight, which had fluctuated as frequently as cloud formations, and the fact that I could look at every photograph of myself taken since 2009 and tell her, to the pound, how much I weighed in each one. I told her about my obsession with alcohol that hadn't waned since I was a teenager, my unquenchable thirst when most people my age knew when to stop, how I'd always been known for knocking it back in record time, the vast black holes in my memory from these nights over the years; my increasing shame and distress over these lost hours and that unrecognizable madwoman running around town who I was supposed to be responsible for, but who I had no recollection of being or ever having been. I told her about my inability to commit to a relationship; my obsession with masculine attention and my simultaneous fear of getting too close to someone. How difficult it was for me to witness all of my friends enter into long-term relationships as if they were lowering themselves into a refreshing swimming pool. How every companion I've ever had has asked why I can't do the same, and how I've always feared that my romantic wiring was flawed.

We discussed how I had distributed myself across as many lives as possible like the last teaspoon of Marmite. I told her that I gave away nearly all of my vitality to other people without being asked. I described the control I believed this gave me over what others thought of me, despite the fact that it made me feel increasingly like a hypocrite. I told her that I fantasized about what others said about me behind my back, and that I would likely concur with almost any insult hurled at me. I told her the lengths I had gone to in order to gain approval: spending all my money on rounds of drinks for people I had never met and not being able to pay my rent the following week; starting Saturday nights at 4:00 p.m. and ending them at 2:00 a.m. in order to attend six different birthday parties of people I scarcely knew. How exhausted and heavy and spineless and self-loathing this had made me feel. The pitiful irony that despite having the largest group of friends surrounding me, I felt I couldn't tell them any of this. How ingrained was my dread of dependence? That I could cry in the bed of a New York stranger, but I couldn't ask my closest companions for assistance.

I stated, "However, none of this is having any discernible effect on my life." "I feel foolish for coming here because the situation could be much worse." I have wonderful companions and a loving family. My work progresses well. From the outside, no one would suspect that anything is amiss with me. I simply feel awful. All the time.'

She stated, "If you feel like crap all the time, it has a tremendous impact on your life."

"I suppose."

'You feel like you're going to fall because you're broken into a hundred various floating pieces,' she told me. You're scattered everywhere. You have no rooting. You lack the ability to be with yourself.' Finally, the back wall of my irises gave way, and tears began to flow from the deepest well in the pit of my stomach.

"I feel as though nothing holds me together anymore," I told her, my shortness of breath punctuating my sentences like hiccups and the tears streaming freely down my cheekbones as hot as blood.
'Of course you do,' she stated with a softer tone. "You have no sense of self,"

Consequently, this explains why I was present. The penny finally fell. I believed I had a dread of falling, but in reality I lacked identity. And the things I used to use to occupy that void were no longer effective; they only made me feel further from myself. This overwhelming anxiety was in the mail. This diagnosis startled me, as I believed my sense of self to be rock-solid. This is what my generation, Generation Self-Awareness, does. Since 2006, we have been filling out 'About Me' sections. I believed I took the most thoughtful photographs of anyone I knew. Just as I was about to leave, she said, "You will never know what I truly think of you," letting me know she had already figured out how I operate. You may be able to deduce from my demeanor whether I like you, but you will never know what I think of you personally. You must let go of that notion if we are to make any progress.
Initially, I felt apprehensive paranoia, followed by an almost instantaneous sense of relief. She told me to cease making stupid jokes. She was telling me to quit apologizing for using all of the Kleenex on the table next to me. She was indicating that this was a room in which I did not have to carefully craft every word, gesture, and anecdote in the hopes that she would like me. This woman with no sense of self, no self-respect, and no self-esteem – a shapeshifting, people-pleasing presence; an anxious bundle – was granted permission to simply exist. She was telling me I was secure to let go in this room just behind Oxford Circus, with the cream carpet and the burgundy sofa. I departed her office and walked the 5.5 miles to my residence. I was simultaneously relieved to have finally found my way to that room and weighed down by the weight of what was to come. I told myself that in three months, everything would be resolved.

On the following Friday, I told Eleanor that India said she didn't want me to undergo this procedure out of concern that it would make me sad. I told her I partially concurred. Thus began the procedure.

Each week, we conducted self-investigations to answer the question of how I became who I was after twenty-seven years. We conducted a forensic investigation of my past, discussing occurrences as recent as the night before and as far back as a twenty-year-old PE class. Therapy is a massive excavation of your psyche until something is uncovered. It's a weekly intimate episode of Time Team, a collaboration between the therapist Mick Aston and the patient Tony Robinson. We conversed until she presented a plausible cause-and-effect theory; then, most importantly, we determined how to modify it. Occasionally, she assigned me things to attempt, tasks to complete, questions to answer, ideas to ponder, and conversations to have. For two months, every Friday afternoon I wept. I slept ten hours every Friday evening.

The common misconception about therapy is that it is all about placing culpability on others; however, as the weeks passed, I discovered the opposite to be true. I've heard of therapists who took on a sort of defensive, delusional mother role in their patients' lives, constantly assuring them that it was not their fault, but the boyfriend's, the boss's, or the best friend's. I detested our sessions because Eleanor rarely allowed me to deflect responsibility to others and always forced me to consider what I had done to end up in a particularly dire situation. 'Unless someone dies,' she told me one Friday, 'if something terrible happens in a relationship, you have played a part in it.' A couple of months into our relationship, Eleanor and I shared our first genuine laughter. I arrived in shambles after a difficult work week. I was low on funds and self-esteem, concerned about paying my rent, and concerned that my career was stagnating.

My paranoia was out of control; I imagined that every employer I had ever had believed I was incompetent, untalented, and worthless. I stayed in my apartment for three days. I described to her a vivid fantasy in which a boardroom full of strangers discussed what a dreadful and inept writer I was. While I spoke, her expression contorted in disbelief as she observed me. Although my closest companions were supportive of the process, it soon became clear that self-examination made me uninterested in the wrong people. I began to drink less and less, constantly questioning whether I was doing it for pleasure or as a means of avoiding a problem. I attempted to stop people-pleasing because I realized that giving so much of my time and energy away was what was chipping away at the void I did not want to turn into a quarry. I was more truthful; I told people when I was upset, offended, or furious, and I valued the sense of serenity that came with having integrity, even if it meant having an awkward conversation. I became more self-aware, and consequently, I made less of a fool of myself for the amusement of others.

I felt like I was growing week by week; I could feel my insides photosynthesizing each day that I implemented new routines. I developed an obsession with houseplants, a type of pathetic green fallacy. I researched what I should place in every corner of light and shade, and I filled my apartment with an abundance of greenery: pothos plants crawled down bookshelves, a Boston fern perched atop my refrigerator, and a Swiss cheese plant fanned against my bedroom's bright, white wall. I hung a flawless philodendron above my bed, and at night, a few cold drops of water fell from the leaves' heart-shaped tips onto my scalp. India and Belle questioned whether this was beneficial for me, comparing it to water torture in China. But I had read that it was guttation, a process in which a plant sheds excess water at night; it exerts great effort to free itself of anything exerting pressure on its roots. And I told them that it was significant to me. Together, the philodendron and I were doing something.

When I drank less, I experienced the novel sensation of waking up with a linear memory of the previous night. The things people said, the way they looked, and the signals they believed were private between one another. I noticed that whenever I turned up to a social event, people desired the bad stuff. If it was at the bar table, they wanted another bottle of wine, to contact a drug dealer, to sit outside and chain-smoke, or to spread malicious rumors about someone we knew while inebriated. Unknowingly, I had become a black-market trader during a night out. I didn't realize I was everyone's green light for evil behavior until I stopped. Then, around five months into therapy, I felt as though we had abruptly hit a brick wall. My progress reached a plateau. I found myself defending myself against her. She stated that I was combative with her.

In one session, I suggested that perhaps there was no answer to be found in dissecting the events and decisions of my life; in rehashing what happened with that one relationship or what my parents said or didn't say when I was growing up. Perhaps it was an exercise in futility; perhaps I was born this way. Did she believe it was possible I was simply born in this tier? She stared at me in silence. If I messed up that week, I would sometimes plan out the excuse I would give her so she would be lenient. Then I recalled how much I had to pay to see her, how much extra work I had to do to afford it, and what a privilege it was to be able to afford it at all. And what a waste of money it would have been if I had not told her the truth. Some acquaintances in psychoanalysis told me that they were anxious before their sessions because they were trying to come up with something juicy to share with the therapist. I felt exactly the contrary. I frequently pondered what I could conceal from her or how I could alter a story to make it appear less negative than it actually was. But, naturally, she always saw through it. Because I disclosed my working methods to her. And I always resented how well she knew me, bursting into weeping every time she challenged me. Not because I detested her for questioning something I had done, but rather because I disliked myself for doing it.

At six months, I was on the verge of asking, "Well, what makes YOU so f*cking wise about all this?" Now, now. Tell me how flawless YOU are,' a client requests during a session. And I realized I needed a respite from it, but I kept this to myself. She informed me that she sensed some anger'; I assured her that I was alright. I began to reschedule appointments. I was absent for and a half months. When I returned to her, I discovered she was far more understanding than I remembered and I wondered if I had invented her dogged and unforgiving line of inquiry. Perhaps she had become the vacant canvas onto which I projected all the resentment and disapproval I felt for myself. Midway through our hour-long conversation, she asked me why I had ceased coming regularly without first discussing it with her. I considered fabricating an excuse; I considered the money and time I was investing in this and how it was now too late to back out. I believe that part of the issue was that I had reached a point where I could no longer tolerate Eleanor knowing so much about me – my most sacred, embarrassing, humiliating, dreadful, and precious experiences. And I received no information about her in return. Occasionally, I envisaged Eleanor at home; I pondered her life when she wasn't working as a therapist. I wondered what she said about me to her acquaintances and if she had ever read my articles, viewed my social media feeds, or googled me as I had done when I first received an invoice with her full name.

A few weeks later, when she inquired about my progress in therapy, I admitted that I resented not knowing anything about her. I told her that I understood this was the proper exchange, but that I occasionally felt it was unjust. Why was I required to be nude every week while she was always allowed to wear clothing? I eventually learned Eleanor's vernacular. After a particularly tearful session, she would always say, "Take good care," with the emphasis on "good." This meant, "Don't become completely leathered over the weekend." It was also terrible when she said 'Oh boy' when I told her something. But by far the worst was, 'I've been concerned about you this week.' When Eleanor stated that she had been concerned about me that week, it indicated that I had given her a genuine shitshow the previous Friday. I never ceased dreading Fridays, but my dread gradually diminished. Eleanor and I shared more laughter. I told her that sometimes after our sessions, I went directly to Pret and ate a brownie in about five seconds or went to a store and bought a ten-pound piece of junk that I did not require. She stated that I was concerned about her opinion of me, and I concurred. It is not natural to sit in a small room with someone removed from the rest of your life and tell them all your unfiltered, unedited stories – the ones you've never spoken aloud before, the ones you've never told anyone, maybe not even yourself. However, the healthier I became, the less I judged her. Her true form began to emerge before me: a woman who was on my side.

I comprehended when a friend told me that it is the relationship between patient and therapist, not the talking, that facilitates healing. My gradual sense of tranquility and serenity felt like something we were constructing together, like a physical therapist strengthening a muscle. I carried a portion of her with me, and I'm certain I always will. The work aided in the formation of a new understanding of myself that I will never be able to discard and conceal. That's what she termed it: 'the work'. And this has always been the case. My time with Eleanor was demanding, confronting, and difficult. She did not let me off the hook for anything. She prompted me to consider the role I played in everything. After particularly challenging Friday afternoons, I pondered what my life would have been like if I hadn't decided to embark on this journey of self-discovery. Would it have been simpler to continue being a drunken moron in a taxi speeding down the M1 at 4:00 a.m.? A person whose behavior was never analyzed, but was brushed aside and then repeated the following weekend?

Eleanor enjoyed telling me that existence is crap. She informed me weekly. She told me I would be disappointed. She reminded me that I had no control over the situation. I accepted this inevitability with calm. As our one-year anniversary approached, our conversations began to flow with greater ease; she suggested literature she thought I would find useful. She typically said "Goodbye" instead of "Take care." She ceased saying 'Oh no' in a concerned way when I told her a story and I started hearing a genuinely ecstatic 'Well, this all sounds GREAT!' fairly regularly. One Friday, I ran out of things to say to her. I had no idea how long I wished to remain there or how liberated I desired to feel. But I knew that the longer I stayed, the more the pieces fell into place. I achieved harmony through self-talk, just as she had predicted. I noticed the patterns; I connected the connections. The dialogue began to connect with the action.

The disparity between how I felt on the inside and how I acted shrunk. When things went wrong, I learned to sit with them, to delve profoundly and uncomfortably within myself, as opposed to embarking on a journey to the Outer Hebrides of Experience. The frequency of drinking decreased, and when it did occur, it was for celebration rather than escape, so the outcome was never catastrophic. I felt more steady and robust. The doors within me unlocked one by one, and I empty the rooms of all my s**t and walked her through every piece of old s**t I discovered; I then discarded everything. Every room I unlocked brought me closer to my goal. Calmness is essential to a sense of self. And a sense of belonging.

CHAPTER 22
Heartache Hotel

Before 7 a.m. I awoke to three missed calls from Fairly and a message asking me to contact her. Before I could reach her number again, she called again. I suspected it was subpar. I reflected on the eighteen months since Florence's death and the manner in which Farly had withdrawn from her closest friends and buried her sorrow in the distance. How I had attempted to bring her back to me; to find the right words to comfort her. Whenever we laughed about something and I caught a glimpse of her former self, her laughter would turn into guttural sobbing and she would apologize for her inability to comprehend how her mind and body were functioning. I had only one selfish thought: I have no idea how I'll get her through this again. I inhaled deeply and then picked up the phone. When I arrived an hour later, Farley was alone in their apartment; Scott had left for work, and her employer had granted her a few days of compassionate leave. She recounted the conversation they had the night before in minute detail.

She told me she hadn't seen this coming, that the wedding was the least of her concerns at the moment, and that she would do anything to save her relationship. Because her father and stepmother were spending the weekend in Cornwall, we decided to drive there so that she and Scott could have time apart to reflect. We devised a strategy for what she would say to him over the phone. She asked if I could sit in the same room as her when he called – she was a nervous disaster and wanted to have me in her eyeline to steady herself. I sat on their sofa as she paced around their apartment on the phone, and I admired the home they shared and the life they had created together. There was a photo of them in their early and mid-twenties, holding each other affectionately; it was from their last vacation with Florence. The burnt-orange rug I assisted them in selecting, and the sofa on which we drank red wine until dawn while viewing election results on television. The Morrissey print we purchased for their engagement is displayed on their wall.

I had a peculiar and challenging notion. For so many years, this was my only desire. I used to hope that, at some point, one of them would move on from the other, and that I'd regain my closest friend. But now that time had arrived, I felt nothing but heartbreaking melancholy and longing for her. They had endured so much together, and I desperately wanted them to succeed. We all viewed the upcoming wedding of Fairly and Scott as a form of Polyfilla for the void left in their family. Whenever her family or any of our friends discussed what the day would be like, we all agreed that it would be filled with soaring joy and unavoidable sorrow, but that it would mark the beginning of a new chapter in their lives. A beginning as opposed to an end.

After Florence's passing, I assumed the position of her lady of honor as if it were a knighthood. AJ, Lacey, and I planned a bachelorette party with the same scope and ambition as the Olympic Opening Ceremony. After months and months of begging and negotiating, an East London hotel gave us their top-floor function room overlooking the city at a highly discounted rate to host a large dinner. I arranged for the London Gay Men's Chorus to perform a surprise set of wedding-themed songs for Farly while donning T-shirts bearing her image. I collaborated with a mixologist to create The Farly. I ordered a life-size cardboard cutout of Scott from eBay and affixed a photo of his visage to it so that people could take photos with him. I recorded scores of video messages from people wishing her a happy marriage to play on the night as a This Is Your Life-style video message (VT). These individuals included Dean Gaffney from the 1990s EastEnders, two cast members from Made in Chelsea, the lad with whom she lost her virginity, and the manager of her local dry cleaners. I drifted back into her discussion with Scott. She said, "Perhaps the wedding was too large." "Do you know? Perhaps we allowed the wedding to become chaotic. Perhaps we should just forget about everything and concentrate on ourselves. I received an email at that precise moment from the office of Farly's municipal representative.

I removed it discreetly. We drove to my apartment, where I threw a few things in a bag and texted India and Belle to inform them that Farly had tonsillitis and Scott was out of town for business, so I would be staying with her for a few days. As everything was still so uncertain and no definitive decision had been made, it was best to keep things vague so she could avoid asking any questions. I posted an out-of-office message and we left for Cornwall in her car. It was a trip we had taken together numerous times: M25, M4, M5. For vacations at the house in Cornwall, for the summer road excursions we took when we were sixteen and seventeen, and for the commutes from London to Exeter when we attended Exeter University. Farley had a rigorous ranking system for all motorway service stations based on their snack locations, and she enjoyed putting me to the test (Chieveley, Heston, Leigh Delamere).

Strangely, a lengthy automobile trip seemed to be exactly what we needed at that moment. Our adolescent relationship was rooted in her car. During the years I yearned to be an adult, Farly's driver's license was our passport to freedom. It was our first shared apartment and our refuge from the outside world. There was a hilltop vantage point in Stanmore that provided an Oz-like view of the city. We would drive there after school while listening to Magic FM and sharing a sachet of Silk Cut and a tub of Ben & Jerry's. The journey – five hours – felt even longer than usual. I could hear the noise in Farly's cranium, perhaps because the silence wasn't accompanied by chitchat, radio, or our scratched Joni Mitchell CDs. We placed her cell phone on the dashboard and awaited Scott's call informing us of his dreadful error. Every time her phone beeped, her eyes momentarily shifted from the road to the display.

"Check it for me," she would swiftly request. It was always another message from a friend wishing her and her tonsillitis a speedy recovery and asking if they could bring her soup and periodicals.
"For fuck's sake," she said with a feeble chuckle.
I offered, "At least you know you're loved." There was additional uneasy silence.
She inquired, "What am I going to tell everyone?" "Every single wedding guest"
I said, "You don't have to consider that just yet." And if that situation does occur, you won't be required to disclose anything. We can do everything for you.

She said, "I don't know how I could survive this without you." As long as I have you, things will be fine.

I told her, "I'm right here," or "I'm present." "I won't be going anywhere. I'll be right here forever, buddy. And we will reach the other side together, regardless of how this place appears.'

As she stared directly ahead into the darkness of the M5, she shed tears.

Dolly, I'm regretful if I ever made you feel like a second-class citizen.

Richard and Annie were awake and awaiting our arrival shortly after midnight. I made tea – in the week following Floss's death, I memorized how everyone took theirs, as it was the only useful thing I could do – and we sat on the sofa to discuss the implications of everything that had been said.

I and Farley slept in the same bed with the lights off.

Do you know what the true tragedy of this situation is?

She said, "Continue"

"Lauren and I have perfected the chords and harmonies of "One Day Like This" for the ceremony."

Oh, I realize, don't. I adored the audio file you sent me.

The string quartet has just certified that they can perform the introduction.

"I am fully aware"

I said, "It could be a blessing in disguise." I believe everyone now associates this tune with X Factor montages.

"Are you going to lose money on the bachelorette party?"

I said, "Don't worry about any of that." We'll resolve the issue. In the darkness, there was silence, and I waited for her next statement.

She said, "Continue" I am ninety percent certain that it is not occurring at this time, so you might as well tell me.

However, will it make you sad?

No, it will make me feel better.

I informed her of the weekend plans we had made for her. She grumbled like a child deprived of candy whenever she encountered absurdity. On my phone, we viewed videos of the Great and the Good of Britain's D-List sending their well wishes.

She said, "Thank you for planning it." It would have been great had it occurred. I would have cherished it.

We'll do it again for you all.

I will never marry again.

"You are unaware of that. And even if you don't, I'll transfer all those plans to a birthday in a lazy manner. I'll make your fortieth memorable. Years of bed-sharing and bickering over her falling asleep before the conclusion of a film had taught me that she was dozing off when I heard her breathing deep and slow. I said, "Wake me in the middle of the night if you need me."

Thank you, Ladies. Sometimes I wish we could just be in a relationship,' she stated sleepily. Everything would be simplified.

Yes, but I'm afraid you're not my type, Farly.

She laughed and then wept a few minutes later. I caressed her back while remaining silent. The next few days were spent taking lengthy walks and discussing the same details of their previous conversation in an attempt to determine where things may have gone wrong. I prepared tea that Farly did not drink, Richard prepared meals that she scarcely consumed, and we watched television as she stared into the distance. A few days later, I had to return to London for business. A few days later, Farly also returned to the city, where she and Scott agreed to walk and discuss the situation in their local park.

On the morning of their scheduled meeting, I was unable to concentrate and glued to my phone, expecting a message from her. After three hours, I finally decided to call her. She answered the phone before the first ring had concluded. "It's over," she exclaimed abruptly. "Inform everyone that the wedding has been canceled. I will contact you later. I called each of our close acquaintances individually and relayed the news; each was as shocked as the last. I sent a carefully formulated message to Farly's side of the guest list explaining that the wedding was canceled. Then it was concluded. A copy-pasted message in an email and a few phone calls extinguished the fire. That day, in that future, their story concluded. I canceled her elaborate bachelorette party, which was scheduled to take place in less than a month. Everyone I contacted, who was already aware that the wedding had been postponed a year due to a family calamity, had nothing but condolences to offer. Farly left the apartment the day of their conversation and traveled a few miles to Annie and Richard's family residence. I went to the home with a depleted positivity account and well into my overdraft of uplifting platitudes.

She told me, "I feel like I'm in jail for something I didn't do." "I feel as if my existence is over there, but I'm locked up over here and told I can't reach it. I desire my previous lifestyle.
You will arrive at your destination. It won't always be this way, I promise.
I am doomed.
"No," I replied. "You are not afflicted. You have had a horrendous, horrible, unbearable run of poor luck. You have experienced more darkness in eighteen months than many people experience in a lifetime. But you have so much light ahead of you; you must cling onto that.
"This is what everybody said after Florence passed away. I don't believe I can endure much more.

With everyone's encouragement, Farley immediately returned to work, and our colleagues initiated a military operation to keep her preoccupied. Even though it was the most time we'd spent together since we were adolescents, I sent her a postcard every other day so she'd always have something pleasant to look forward to when she got home from work. For her bachelorette party, the attendants took her to the countryside for a weekend of wine tasting and cooking. I arranged a vacation for the week of her wedding in Sardinia. In the month following their breakup, we all took turns spending the evenings with her after work; not a single night passed without at least one of us being present. Sometimes we discussed what was occurring, and other times we simply ate Lebanese takeout and watched vulgar television. Whoever visited would convey a message to the rest of us on their way home, updating us on her condition and inquiring as to who would be her next visitor. We were a group of caretakers; on-duty nurses. Our first-aid kit consisted of Maltesers and Gogglebox episodes. During this time, I was reminded of the chain of support that keeps a sufferer afloat: the person at the center of a crisis requires the support of their family and closest friends, while these individuals require the support of their friends, partners, and family. Then even those who are twice removed may need to discuss it with someone. It requires an entire community to mend a broken heart. Farly and I drove back to her apartment and waited in the car while she retrieved additional belongings and had a final conversation with Scott. Their apartment was listed for sale. Farly unpacked everything into her childhood bedroom, a place that was more than transient but not permanent.

The first time any of us saw a glimmer of Farly's former self was on a Sunday when I convinced my friends to participate in a photo session for a fake dinner party. The editor wanted a photo of me 'entertaining guests' in my apartment to accompany an article I had written for a newspaper's culture section about the demise of the traditional dinner party. I had informed him that I did not have any male acquaintances available on that particular day, and he reluctantly agreed that an all-female gathering was acceptable. However, when the photographer arrived, it seemed he was under new instruction to absolutely make sure there were men in the photo. Farly, who had been guzzling white wine since her arrival at noon, went door-to-door on my street in an unsuccessful attempt to locate a male neighbor. Meanwhile, Belle and AJ drove to our local pub, entered, tapped a glass for everyone's attention, and made a rather weak announcement that they were looking for a few males to be photographed in exchange for slow-roasted lamb and their picture in the newspaper.

Belle yelled, "If this sounds like something you would be interested in, then the red Seat Ibiza will be waiting outside."
Five minutes later, a group of disheveled, intoxicated men in their thirties and forties stumbled out of the bar and into the car. When we were all crammed around the table, clinking our glasses and attempting to look like old friends, it was evident that one of the gentlemen was significantly more inebriated than the others, devouring the roast lamb with his hands like a Roman emperor. In my rather crowded living room, where the photographer was standing on a chair to get everyone in the frame, a light bulb burst and one of the men began shouting for more wine. It resembled a slapstick comedy with people running around and objects shattering with a low level of manic energy.

I murmured to the ladies, "This is a disaster," as I walked away.
Farley barked inebriated, "Oh, I don't think it's a catastrophe AT ALL." A month ago, my partner of seven years dumped me, so this is a piece of cake! The photographer gazed at me for reassurance, and even the intoxicated emperor ceased chewing. "Cheers!" she exclaimed, lifting her glass to toast us all. We soon learned how to respond to this type of suicide bomb joke, which became a well-worn

fixture in our conversations with Farly. You couldn't participate in the banter because you didn't know where the black humor ended and cruelty began, but you also couldn't disregard it. You simply had to guffaw out loud. A few days prior to what would have been Farly's nuptials, we departed for Sardinia. We landed late and drove to the north-west of the island in an uninsured rental car, gingerly winding up coastal roads while listening to the same Joni Mitchell album from our first road trip over ten years prior. A time when even a relationship seemed absurdly impossible, let alone a wedding cancellation.

It was sufficient that we stayed in a hotel with a pool, a bar, and a room with a view of the ocean. Farly, the school-obsessed girl who went on to become a teacher, is and has always been a creature of habit, and we soon developed our own. Before breakfast, we would exercise on the shore in the bright, early-morning sunlight and then swim in the ocean. So, I would swim. Farly would observe from the dunes. When it comes to outdoor swimming, Farly and I have the greatest difference of opinion; I'll strip off at the sight of nearly any body of open water, whereas Farly only swims in chlorinated pools.

"Come on," One morning, when the sea was as calm and balmy as bathwater, I yelled at the shore. "You have to come in!" It is so beautiful.'
'But what if there are fish?' she bellowed at me with a grimace.
"There are no fish here!" I hollered. Okay, there might be some seafood.
She shouted back, "You know I'm afraid of fish."
"How can you be afraid of them when you consume them?"
I dislike the notion of them swimming around beneath me.
I exclaimed, "You sound so bloody suburban, Farly!" You don't want to lose out on life because you only shop in shopping centers for fear of rain ruining your blow-dry and only swim in pools for fear of fish.
"We live in a suburb, Dolly. That is precisely what we are.
"Go on!" It's normal! It's God's very own pool! It's curative! God dwells in the sea!f
She stood up and rubbed the sand off her legs before declaring, "If there's one thing I know for certain, it's that there is no God, Doll!" She joyously yelled it while paddling into the ocean.

We would spend the entire morning reading and listening to music before having our first drink of the day at noon. We slept all afternoon in the sun, then showered and went out to dinner with our tans. We would then return to the hotel, consume Amaretto Sours on the terrace in the evening heat, play cards, and send tipsy postcards to our friends. Farley awoke before I did on the day of the nuptials. She was observing the ceiling.

Are you okay? I inquired as soon as I opened my eyes.
She replied, "Yes," before turning away and raising the bed's cover.
"I just want today to end," she said.
I stated that today would be one of the most difficult days. "Then it will be concluded. At midnight, the task is completed. And you will never have to endure it again.'
Yes, she replied softly. I sat on her bed's footboard.
I inquired, "What do you want to do today?" I've reserved a table at a restaurant with glowing five-star TripAdvisor reviews that include disgusting close-up photographs of the food as if it were a crime scene.
"That sounds good," she sighed. "I think all I want to do is lie on a sun lounger like a simple whore."

We spent the majority of the day in solitude, reading our books and listening to podcasts with earplugs. She would occasionally glance around and remark, "Right now, I would be having breakfast with my bridesmaids or putting on my wedding dress." She checked the time on her phone in the middle of the afternoon.

"The score in England is 10 to 4." In precisely ten minutes, I would have been wedded.
"Yeah, but at least you're sunbathing in beautiful Italy instead of floating down a lake with your father in rainy Oxfordshire," the speaker said.
"I was never going to arrive on a gondola," she exclaimed with exasperation. I only mentioned it as a prospective option because the venue said that some of the other brides had done so.
However, you did contemplate it.
"No, I did not."

Yes, because when you told me about it, I could hear in your voice that you were waiting for me to respond positively.

"No, I was not!"

It would have been extremely awkward if everyone had been gazing at you while you floated down a lake in a massive dress, followed by someone yanking you out of it and a sailor clattering about with oars.

"It lacked a sailor," she murmured. And it was devoid of oars.

I entered the bar and placed an order for a bottle of Prosecco.

Right, I said as I poured the ice-cold champagne into plastic flutes by the pool. "You would have been exchanging vows at this time. I believe we should exchange vows.

"For whom?"

'To ourselves,' I said. And to one another

She said, "Okay," as she placed her sunglasses on top of her cranium. You will go first.

I stated, "I promise not to judge how you handle this when we get home." "It's acceptable if you want to go through a really intense amphetamine and casual sex phase. It is acceptable if you confine yourself in your home for a year. You have my support no matter what you decide to do, because I cannot fathom what it must be like to lose the loved ones you have.

She said "thank you" while sipping her Prosecco and halting to reflect. "I promise to always allow you to develop. I will never claim to know your true identity simply because we've known each other since childhood. I recognize that you are undergoing a period of significant change, and I will always encourage that.

I remarked, "That's a good one," as I clinked her glass. "Alright, I promise to always inform you when you have something stuck in your teeth."

"Always," the speaker exclaimed.

Particularly as we age and our gums begin to recede. That's when the verdant greens can really get lodged.'

She said, "Don't make me more depressed than I already am."

Make a promise to yourself.

She said, "I promise to never lose sight of my friends if I fall in love again." I will never forget how indispensable you all are and how much we rely on one another.

On the evening of Farly's wedding reception for over two hundred guests, we took a taxi to a restaurant on a cliff overlooking the ocean.

She said, "You would have been delivering your speech at this time."
Did you ever compose it?
"No," I replied. When I've been a bit inebriated and emotional, I've jotted down some ideas for it in the notes section of my iPhone. But I had not yet written it down.'
I wonder if I would have been joyful throughout the entire day or if any of it would have been stressful.

After Florence's death, I recalled an article I had read about premature death, in which an agony aunt advised a grieving father not to consider the life his teenage son would have led had he not been killed in a car accident. This fantasy, she stated, was a torturous exercise rather than a soothing one.
I said, "You know, that life isn't happening elsewhere." It does not exist in any other dimension. The length of your relationship with that man was seven years. That was it, that was the end of it.
"I know"
"Your life is happening now." You are not about to live a carbon copy of it.'
Yes, I suppose it would be best not to dwell on what might have been.
Don't compare it to Sliding Doors.
I adore this film.
And thank God it's not because no one could ever carry off Gwyneth Paltrow's blonde haircut.
Fairly stated flatly, "I'd look like Myra Hindley," while signaling for another carafe of wine. Did you have any reservations about me and him?
"Do you want to know the truth?"
"Yes, I do," she responded. "It doesn't matter now, but I'd still like to know."
"Yes," I replied. "I grew to truly love him, and I believed there was a future in which you could find great happiness."
She observed the setting sun, which was balanced on the horizon of the deep-blue Mediterranean like a flawless peach.
"I appreciate you never telling me,"
The sun was absorbed by the sea, and as if on a dimmer switch, the sky gradually darkened to a dusky blue and then to night. It never got worse than that day again.

We drove to another coastal town where we met Sabrina and Belle after a week together. The remainder of the vacation was spent drinking Aperol, playing cards, and lounging on the beach. Belle and I left the apartment at six a.m. one morning, stripped at the beach and swam nude in the light of the sunrise. As anticipated, Farley had good days and quiet days during our final week together. We all spoke extensively about what had transpired, the underlying cause for the holiday. However, she also began discussing the future rather than the past, including where she was going to reside and her new daily routine. Over the course of the fortnight it felt like she shed one of her skins of melancholy. One night, she got so drunk – more drunk than she had been since we were teenagers – that she began flirting with the manager of a local restaurant who resembled a sixty-something Italian John Candy. This is the most recognizable rite of passage and a sign that you've entered a new phase of getting over a breakup.

When we returned to London, we noticed a significant shift in the atmosphere. Her 29th birthday marked three months since I awoke to three missed calls that morning. It felt like a significant occasion, so we celebrated by dining at one of our favorite taverns and then going out dancing. She wore the dress I found for the never-held bachelorette party. It was black, cut low on each side, and revealed a tattoo she received when she was nineteen, which was a disastrous, impulsive decision made in a Watford tattoo parlor. Two small stars, one colored in pink and the other in ill-considered yellow (her mother exclaimed in despair, "A Jew with a yellow star tattooed on her!"). On the afternoon of her birthday, she visited another tattoo parlor to correct a mistake she made a decade prior. She filled in the stars with a dark pigment; she painted it black. She placed a 'F' next to Florence's name and a 'D' next to mine. A reminder that no matter what we lose, no matter how uncertain and unpredictable life becomes, there are those who will walk alongside us forever.

CHAPTER 23
I Got Gurued

I was asked to write a first article for a magazine about the perils of people-pleasing during the early summer of Farly's sorrow. The editor for whom I was working suggested that I speak with the author of a new book on the subject. His name was David, he was nearing fifty; he was an actor turned writer. Before we spoke on the phone, I googled him and discovered that he was also very handsome, with olive complexion, salt-and-pepper hair, and gentle brown eyes. The PDF of the book sent to me by the publisher was a frustratingly brilliant read. His work centered on the human need for approval and how it hinders pleasure. It felt as though someone or something had seized my shoulders with a pair of strong, dependable hands and given me a vigorous, much-needed shake.

We exchanged emails for some time before arranging a time to speak. His voice was significantly more pronounced and dramatic than I had anticipated. His general aura resembled that of a true hippie, but he spoke like a member of the RSC ensemble. I asked him about the book and the ideas that had stayed with me the most, and he said that as children, we are continuously told to control our behavior. He described how being told not to be domineering, not to show off, or not to be a clever-clogs erects barriers around certain facets of our personality, and we fear revisiting them as adults. Instead, we conceal those aspects of ourselves that are dark, loud, eccentric, or twisted out of dread of not being accepted. He argued that these aspects of ourselves were the most attractive. Because the article was written from a personal perspective, we were required to discuss my own experiences. I disclosed that I began seeing a therapist this year.

"The danger of someone like you engaging in therapy is that you appear intelligent," he said. "You will understand the theory of everything very readily. In conversation, you can be academic about yourself. But, you know, all that chatter will only get you so far. This transformation must be felt deeply in your essence. It cannot be limited to topics discussed with a therapist. You must feel it in the backs of your knees, in your womb, in your toes, and in your extremities,' he said as his voice slowed. I responded, "Hmm," in accord. We conversed for approximately 45 minutes, ranging from passages in the book to his years of research and work to my own experiences. He addressed me without any formalities or civility. I felt as if he had reached my inner equator through a simple telephone call. I had the impression that he was flirting with me, but I couldn't tell if he was speaking to me so intimately for the purpose of obtaining excellent quotes for the article. By the end of our conversation, it no longer felt like an interview but more like a casual conversation. I could sense he also wanted to know if I was in a relationship, but I remained vague on this point. He stated that he believed I could benefit from a one-on-one session with him.

A few months later, as I was returning late from a party, I received a WhatsApp message from David. He told me he was on vacation in France and had just returned from a long walk under the stars when he abruptly recalled that he hadn't seen our interview anywhere.
This is undoubtedly my narcissism speaking – when will the essay be published?
Not at all narcissistic, I responded. It has been delayed for one issue, we apologize. I will text you the day it is released next month. If you are not in the country, I can mail you a copy.
"I will return by then. How are you doing?' he inquired. The last time we spoke, you seemed to be on the verge of something.
I typed, "Still on the verge of something." Still attempting to transition into a new paradigm. Easy as pie. How do you do?'
'Same.'
He informed me that he had recently ended a very long-term relationship. He believed that an amicable and mutual separation was appropriate. He told me that sometimes a breakup is nothing but a relief for both parties, like when the air conditioner's low, constant hum is eventually turned off and you don't notice it until everything is silent. We learned about each other's fundamentals through hours of texting that night, which we had not garnered from our initial conversation. We both grew up in North London and attended conservative boarding institutions, which is why I suspected he disliked his voice as much as I disliked mine. He had four children, two boys and two girls, and he was evidently devoted to each one. I

could identify a man using his children as a pick-up line from a mile away; this was not one of those instances. He knew every tiny detail of each child's character and passions and aspirations and daily life and he talked about all of them with genuine fascination and devotion.

We discussed music and song lyrics. I told him that my favorite singer was John Martyn and that his music was the only relationship I'd ever had with a man that endured more than a few years. He told me a story about how he purchased one of John Martyn's guitars from his ex-wife and offered it to me because he could sense how much I adored his music. We discussed a book we'd both read that had converted me to vegetarianism; we were both angered by the same statistics and passages. We discussed our boyhood vacations in France. We discussed our parents. We discussed the rain. I told him that I adored it more than clear heavens and bright sunshine. I described how the rain had always comforted and soothed me, and how, as a child, I would ask my mother if I could remain in the trunk of her parked car when it rained. When I read in Rod Stewart's autobiography that he would stand in the middle of the street with his arms outstretched every time it poured in Los Angeles because he missed England so much, I realized I could never leave England. We said our goodbyes at 3 a.m. The following morning, I felt as though I was recuperating from a vivid dream. But sure enough, there was a new message from David waiting for me on my phone like a gleaming pound coin left by the tooth fairy.

I was required to inform my acquaintances about David because I never hung up the phone with him. We exchanged messages from the instant we awoke until we went to bed. I devoted approximately five hours per day to working, dining, and washing, but even during those times, I thought about him. Sabrina told me that she could tell I was glued to my phone screen during our lunch together. My friends thought I was insane for becoming so rapidly obsessed with someone I had never met. But they were also accustomed to it; me finding a new romantic interest had always been like a ravenous child unwrapping Christmas presents. I ripped open the packaging, became frustrated trying to make it work, played with it obsessively until it broke, and then threw the fragments of plastic away on Christmas

Day. I emailed Farley the recording of the initial interview between myself and David. "Listen here," I scrawled. Then you will comprehend why I'm behaving so crazy about this man. An hour later, I received a response to my email from her. It read, "Okay, I understand why you're acting so crazy about this man." A week after we began messaging, we had a phone conversation. Due to the altered relationship between interviewer and interviewee, everything felt different compared to the last time we spoke months ago.

Another week passed with thousands of messages and dozens of phone calls. I became increasingly intrigued by him, and I desired to know his opinions on everything. No detail was overlooked; I was captivated by the minuteness of our conversation. On any topic that piqued my interest, he had something new to say. I felt revitalized and refreshed when this man's interest shone on me. There were insufficient hours in the day to speak with David. I required more, more, and more. Soon, messages and phone calls were insufficient. We exchanged our entire bodies of work. He sent me unpublished chapters from his new book, and I sent him articles and screenplays in draft form. We told each other the things we wouldn't know from talking and googling for photographs – that my nails were always bitten down from my anxious disposition, that his fingertips were hard from playing guitar. I watched the short films he had appeared in with rapt attention; I thought he was a genius and told him so, noting memorable lines and shots that I adored and contacting him to discuss them.

"Go look at the moon," he instructed me over the phone late one evening. I slid on my sneakers and put on a coat over my T-shirt and knickers. I walked to the end of my street before entering Hampstead Heath. He told me about a woman he once dated who lived in Highgate and gave him a thirty-second head start before chasing him through the Heath at night. They had intercourse against an oak tree in the woods. I sat on a bench on a vantage point overlooking the city, stretched my bare legs out under the moonlight, and told him about another bench I had seen here that had made me weep when I read the inscription carved into it. In remembrance of Wynn Cornwell, who swam there well into her nineties, I swam all summer in the meadow adjacent to the Ladies' Pond. I was aware that I was investing a significant amount of time and effort in a total stranger, but I had every reason to trust him. I counted down the days until there was nothing but air between us, and in the interim, I relished this place of our own making; he was a portal at the side entrance of my mundane daily life that allowed me to enter a magical, technicolor world. If I had a dilemma, I would seek his counsel. If I was having trouble finding the end of a sentence while composing, I would seek his opinion.

One afternoon, he texted me, "Thanks for being more forthcoming with me." It's seductive. Obviously, I would continue doing nearly anything if a man I admired told me it was seductive. We frequently remarked on the strangeness of the intensity of our communication; for him, it was wholly novel and peculiar. I had never formed such a strong connection with someone I had never met, but I was accustomed to speaking with strangers due to my formative years on MSN and subsequent years of online dating as an adult. I slept poorly the night before David's return to England. The day after he was to drop off his children at their mother's house, drive to London, and spend the night at a friend's, we had a perfect date planned. I planned to meet him on Hampstead Heath in the early afternoon with a bottle of wine and two plastic glasses as the weather was favorable. India and Belle assisted me in selecting an outfit: a blue tea dress and white sneakers. I tidied my dwelling. I stocked up on quality bread for the inevitable morning after. However, I had to go on a date the night before our afternoon appointment. A matchmaking service wanted me to write about them in my dating column. It was organized weeks before David and I began our virtual relationship, and it made perfect sense at the time – they needed the exposure, and I required a date and a copy. I didn't want to abandon the unfortunate man, so we arranged to meet for an early evening drink in a central location. I knew I could return home by nine o'clock.

David's final words to me were, "Call me later, you heartbreaker." I turned out to be anything but a heartbreaker; quite the contrary, in fact. As I've observed in the majority of situations, neither of us wished to be there. I was infatuated with a man I had never met, whereas he was still in love with an ex-girlfriend with whom he had regrettably botched things up. We shared our respective stories with one another. I told him to go to his ex-girlfriend's house with flowers and tell her he'd never stopped loving her; he told me to go home and get an early night because I was obviously going to meet my future husband the next day. We left after one drink, took the same tube home, and said our goodbyes with an embrace. When I returned home, I called David to inform him of the date. He had driven to London earlier than anticipated and was staying on his friend's sofa in a flat about two miles west of my apartment.

I crept out of the apartment and descended the iron outdoor stairs, and there he stood on my street, his tall, broad silhouette and dark hair visible only in the moonlight. I paused briefly on the stairs to take him in, feeling as though I had just jumped off a cliff and was about to strike the surface of the still water. I rushed up to him, encircled his neck with my arms, and we kissed. The subsequent hours transpired precisely as I had anticipated they would. We drank, conversed, listened to music, and then kissed while lying next to one another. I inhaled his bare, tattooed skin, which was walnut-brown and powdery from the French sun, as well as the aroma of tobacco and earth. I observed his mannerisms that a phone and photograph could not capture, such as the fold of his eyelids and the way an's' slipped between his teeth. He listened to me closely, he talked to me directly; I was open and trusting and marveled at my ability to experience such intimacy with someone I barely knew.

"Do you know what's funny?" he asked with a head kiss.
'What?'
"You are exactly as I expected you to be. Like the child who shields her eyes with her hands on the playground and believes no one can see her.

What does that mean?
He said, "You can't hide from me." I was already aware that I could never lie to this individual. I knew I was in trouble.
"Are you disappointed we didn't go on the ideal date first?" As I transitioned into the dreamy, mumbling wasteland between consciousness and slumber, I inquired.
No, he replied while caressing my hair. Not even close. What are your plans for tomorrow?
"Editorial meeting at 1," I stated.
"I could meet you afterward," he proposed.

I closed my eyes and immediately fell into a restful slumber.

A few hours later, a sound woke me. David was dressed and standing at the foot of my bed.

Are you okay? I inquired dozingly.

"I'm fine," he sneered.

"Where are you headed?"

To go for a journey

I checked the time and it was 5:00 a.m.

What -- now?

Yes, I'd enjoy a trip!

"Okay," I responded. "Would you like me to give you my keys so you can re-enter?"

"No," he replied. He knelt beside the bed and kissed my arm from the elbow to the shoulder. "Return to sleep,"

He shut the door. I heard him exit the apartment and drive away in his car. I stared at the white ceiling of my bedroom, attempting to piece together what had happened. I experienced a bitter sense of violent rejection. I felt it from the pit of my stomach to the back of my throat: self-disgust, self-loathing, and self-pity, squared. That's how I felt when Harry called me all those years ago.

Several hours later, I received a message containing a conundrum from David.

"Hey," it stated. Apologies if that was strange; that was a peculiar exit. It was so beautiful to see you and touch you – it sent me deep within, and I felt this chasm between the incredible intimacy we've created over the past few days and the contrary, not "knowing" each other. I observed him typing and refused to respond until I saw something that made sense. It caused me to ponder significant issues. Fuck. I pray you're not in pain, but you may just be saying "Whatever" But perhaps you're strange.' I regarded my phone, uncertain of how to respond. He wrote, "I hope you didn't wake up sad."

"I woke up depressed," I responded. Rarely do I allow others to get near to me.

"I concur. I am truly contrite. It was not a case of abandonment.

I recalled the final call I ever had with Harry. How I pleaded with him to adore me; how I convinced him through tears that I was worthy of his affection. My fingertips turned purple as I listened for any trembling in his voice that might have led me to believe I could desperately cling to him. That was no longer my reality. Not the person I desired to be. I deleted David's number and then deleted his conversations and call history.

I felt a combination of loneliness, embarrassment, grief, and fury as the days passed. I felt like a fool; like a dowdy female character from The Archers who is seduced by a scheming, handsome foreigner before he flees with all her money. To make me feel better, my friends shared similarly humiliating tales of being duped into false intimacy with strangers. One of my dating column's editors forwarded me a 1997 New Yorker article titled "Virtual Love" about the peculiar new phenomenon of falling in love online. The article was written by a female journalist who began a phone and email relationship with a stranger. Two days after David left me in the middle of the night, the magazine published the article that led me to him in the first place. I had entirely forgotten about it, but seeing it in newsstands made me feel as though everything had come full circle. As I had initially promised in the message that sparked this catastrophe, I did not text him to let him know it was available. I never again spoke with David. In the aftermath of the encounter, my companions were in a state of disbelief, with the situation becoming increasingly absurd as time passed. Sometimes, weeks and weeks after the event, India would suddenly set down her glass of wine and exclaim, "Can you BELIEVE that David guy?" as we sat in the pub. Belle considered reporting him for misusing his trusted position.

Some friends believed he was a misogynist who took advantage of a woman with trust issues, got what he wanted, and then departed; a wolf in Glastonbury vendor garb. Others, who were more charitable, believed he was less at ease with the actuality of virtual seduction than a millennial. I was accustomed to conversing with strangers and establishing rapport with them. Meeting them in person for the first time was always jarring, but getting to know someone was simply the art of bridging that distance; he referred to it as a 'chasm'. This is the fundamental concept behind online dating. Helen developed a second theory: that he was experiencing a midlife crisis as a result of his breakup, and that I was merely an impetuous purchase for his ego. After purchasing me, he realized that I would never function for him or fit into his life. But lamenting David's passing would be analogous to a child lamenting the loss of an invisible companion. None of it was authentic. It was hypothetical and fictitious. We played intense chicken with each other, sluts for overblown, artificial sentiment and a desperate need to feel something deep in the dark, damp cellar of ourselves. It consisted of text and spaces. They were pixels. A The Sims game; a dress-up love game. It was engaging in a precisely choreographed dance with satellites.

After hours of analysis, I only now comprehend who David was. He was neither a charlatan, a midlife crisis on the move, nor a caddish Don Juan in Birkenstocks and linen. He was the child on the playground who shielded his eyes and believed no one could see him. But at last I was able to see him, because we were alike; we were both mischievous children. He was disoriented and searching for a lifeboat. He was depressed and required a diversion. We were two lonely individuals in need of an escape fantasy. Perhaps, with a twenty-year age advantage over me, he should have known better, but he didn't. I hope to never again be complicit in such a farce. And I hope that he finds what he is seeking.

CHAPTER 24
Enough

In the weeks after meeting David, I made a loud, defensive declaration of celibacy because I felt exposed and humiliated. Obviously, it was not celibate because, for starters, it lasted less than three months. Second, it was primarily used to attract male attention; it was a type of born-again virgin fantasy test. Which is the exact opposite of what celibacy is intended to accomplish. No nun has ever taken a vow of celibacy, so she appears unattainable. Then followed the calamitous Christmas special. My friends coined the term 'Christmas Special' to characterize a particular type of drunken, carefree fling that occurs only in the days leading up to Christmas, when everyone is high on merriment, goodwill, and advocaat and all bets are off. In the days preceding Christmas, I determined that I deserved an instant dose of validation; a Pot Noodle of self-esteem. I texted a man I'd been chatting with on a dating app for a couple of weeks, a Geordie who worked in the music industry and had a cheeky smile and excellent pick-up lines, after a work party.

He arrived at my apartment at 2:00 a.m. with a bottle of organic red wine, and we made small talk on the settee as if we were two sophisticated metropolitans on an early-evening dinner date rather than two desperate individuals. After precisely one hour of conversation, we began kissing. Then we went to my bedroom and had routine, unremarkable sexual activity. It was the physical equivalent of a rushed sandwich at a highway rest stop – something you believed you were looking forward to, but once you receive it, you question why. Since the night I met Adam in New York, I hadn't had sex with a stranger. I had inadvertently outgrown one-night encounters, like a child who one day decides she no longer wants to play with her Barbies. As soon as it ended, I knew I would never do it again. The sexual activity was enjoyable, but his presence was intolerable.

I once enjoyed the false intimacy of casual intercourse as a student, but it now seems like a farce. This was not at all his fault, but I wanted him out of my apartment, out of my room, and out of my bed with letters from my friends and memory foam mattress topper that I had saved up for. It made me queasy to see the outline of this stranger's sleeping visage in the darkness. The night passed quickly. I awoke with a severe hangover to find Geordie still sleeping in my bed. I had a 'boyfriend experience' man on my hands when he suggested we spend the morning drinking tea and listening to Fleetwood Mac albums while lounging around. I had observed over the years that the 'boyfriend experience' was something certain men offered after a one-night stand in which they behaved in an inappropriately romantic manner the morning after to either make you fall in love with them or to assuage their own feelings of guilt for having sex with someone whose surname they did not know. After spooning you and making you breakfast in the morning, they watched Friends episodes before departing at dusk. They did not call again. It was a presumably free service that concealed a significant emotional cost. I never accepted the 'partner experience' when offered. The following month, my dating column came to an end, leaving me with no justification to always be on the lookout for a new man under the guise of my profession. The end of the column could have easily marked the beginning of a new phase in my life, one that wasn't governed by late-night calls from ex-boyfriends, right-swiping and left-swiping, cornering men at dinner parties, and coordinating cigarette breaks in the bar when an attractive man was outside.

In reality, the column had been a facilitator, but I was the addict. I have always been, even before I was sexually active. Jilly Cooper mentions in her episode of Desert Island Discs that, when she attended an all-girls school, she was so preoccupied with men that she would fantasize about the eighty-year-old male gardener who occasionally worked on the grounds. Growing up, I was that girl, and in a sense, I have never ceased being that girl. I was equally fascinated and frightened by boys; I did not comprehend them and did not wish to. Their purpose was gratification, whereas female companions provided everything else that was significant. It was a method for keeping males at a distance. When Farly and I returned from Sardinia and she began her life as a single woman for the first time since her early twenties, I gave her an authoritative TED lecture on the complexities of contemporary dating. I stated, "The first thing you must realize is that no one meets in person anymore." Since your last appearance on the market, circumstances have shifted, and you have no choice but to adapt.

When it comes to romantic relationships, Farley and I could not be more dissimilar. Farly is a conventional, cohabiting, long-term, committed monogamist. The portion of a relationship that I find the most exhilarating – the unknown, the high-risk, the first few months when you can hardly eat because you have butterflies in your stomach – is the portion that she dislikes the most. That which I dread — barbecues at a boyfriend's family home, two baked potatoes on the couch on a Saturday night in front of the television, and lengthy car trips on the interstate with her — is her idea of heaven. Three months of romance for a lifetime of domesticity, intimacy, practical planning, and roasted potatoes. I would do anything for a lifetime of those first three months on repeat and a guarantee that I would never have to travel with a sexual partner to an Ikea, a National Express coach station, or a relative's residence outside the M25.

This is one of those therapy terms that you pick up along the way. Watch-the-birdie blaming is when you accuse someone else of doing or being precisely what you fear you are in order to deflect responsibility. When it came to Farly's relationship decisions, I did it frequently. I had never realized that my perpetual resistance to commitment was the source of my feeling of confinement; I had always viewed it as a liberating act. Farly may have always felt the need to be in a relationship, but at least she was aware of her desires. I desired something, but I had no notion what it was, and I despised myself for it. Farley and I went for a long walk, during which I told her about my intentions to take a break from sex, including all its preludes and postludes of flirting, texting, dating, and kissing, in an effort to regain my independence. I told her that despite being unmarried for the majority of my life, I had realized that I hadn't been truly single since I was a teenager. She concurred and told me she believed it to be a good concept.

In the days that followed, I couldn't stop thinking about Farly's words; I considered how we'd known each other for twenty years and how I'd never grown tired of her. I reflected on how my affection for her had only intensified as we grew older and shared more experiences. I reflected on how eager I am to share positive news with her or get her perspective during a crisis, and how she remains my favorite partner for dancing. How her value increased, the more history we shared together, like a gorgeous, precious work of art hanging in my living room. Her love surrounded me with a sense of comfort, security, and peace.

I had been led to believe that my value in a relationship rested solely on my sexuality, which explains why I always acted like a caricature nymphomaniac. I had never imagined that a man could love me as much as my peers do, or that I could love a man with the same devotion and care as they do. Perhaps I had been in a wonderful marriage without realizing it. Perhaps Farly was how a healthy relationship feels. I committed myself to abstinence with the intensity of a doctoral student. More I read about sex and love addiction in books, stories, and blogs, the more I realized where I had gone so wrong. Dating had become a source of immediate gratification, an extension of narcissism, and had nothing to do with human connection. I had repeatedly created intensity with men and misconstrued it with intimacy. At JFK, a stranger proposed to me. A mentor of middle age requested that I fly to France to spend a week with him. It was exaggerated, unnecessary, and lacked intimacy with another person. Intensity and closeness. How could I have muddled them up so badly?

A month had passed, and I felt nothing but complete and utter relief. I deleted all courting applications from my cellular device. I purged the numbers I used for prank calls. I stopped responding to ex-boyfriends who would send me messages at 3 a.m. with seemingly casual queries such as 'How's it going, m'lady?' or 'What's the dealio, smith?' I ceased online surveillance of possible conquests and deleted my Facebook account primarily for this reason. I ceased keeping secrets in my life. I halted at the stroke of midnight. I devoted all of my time to my career and connections. Two months went by. I learned what it meant to attend a wedding and truly be present to witness your friends' nuptials, as opposed to treating it like an eight-hour meat market. I discovered what it was like to appreciate the beautiful, bell-like sound of a choir singing in church without frantically scanning the pews to determine which men were unmarried. I learned how to appreciate the conversation of a man seated next to me at dinner regardless of his marital status; to refrain from vying for the attention of the only single man at the table by saying something indecent in a vaguely threatening tone reminiscent of Sid James's bawdiness. I met Leo's new wife for the first time in five years at a party where I also saw him for the first time in five years. I gave them both an embrace and then left them alone.

Harry became engaged, and I felt no resentment whatsoever. Adam moved in with a lady, so I sent him a congratulatory text message. Their stories were irrelevant to me; I no longer required their attention. I felt as though I was finally gaining my own pace and impetus on my own path. I sat on public transportation and immersed myself in my book, rather than attempting to attract the attention of men. I left parties when I wanted to, rather than hopelessly circling the room until the very end in the vain hope of meeting someone I fancied. I didn't go to events just because I knew certain people would be there; I didn't engineer chance encounters with individuals I fancied. I went out dancing with Lauren one night, and when she was accosted, I remained in the middle of the dance floor for an hour, sweating, swaying, and spinning and spinning.

I took two flights to the Orkney Islands in late spring to compose an article about solo travel for a travel magazine. I stayed above a pub that overlooked the port of Stromness, and at night, after enjoying a beer and a steaming bowl of mussels downstairs, I would take a long stroll along the seafront and gaze up at the vast open skies, which were vaster than any sky I had ever seen. One night, having spent a few days in tranquil solitude with my thoughts, I walked under the stars and along the cobbled streets and an idea crept all over me like arresting, vibrant blooms of wisteria. I do not require a dazzlingly charismatic musician to compose a tune about me. I don't need a sage to tell me things I don't know about myself. I do not need to shave my head because a gentleman told me it would look good. I do not need to alter my appearance to be worthy of someone's affection. I do not require a man's words, glances, or comments to believe I am visible; to believe I am present. I do not need to flee from discomfort and into the gaze of a man. This is not where I thrive. Because I am sufficient. My spirit is sufficient. The anecdotes and sentences revolving in my mind are sufficient. I am bubbling, foaming, buzzing, and erupting. I am boiling over and on fire.

My early morning strolls and late night showers are sufficient. My boisterous laughter at the pub is sufficient. My piercing whistling, shower singing, and double-jointed toes are sufficient. I am a freshly poured pint with a substantial foam. I am my own cosmos, galaxy, and solar system. I am the opening act, the primary attraction, and the backup singers. And if this is it, if this is all there is – just me, the trees, the sky, and the oceans – I now realize that it is sufficient. I am adequate. I am adequate. As the words traveled through my body, they shook every cell. I sensed them, I comprehended them, and they merged with my bones. The thought raced and leapt through my body like a thoroughbred. I yelled it into the night sky. I observed my declaration ricochet from star to star, swaying from carbon to carbon like Tarzan. I am complete and whole. I will never be depleted. And I am more than sufficient. (I believe they refer to it as a "breakthrough.")

CHAPTER 25
Twenty-eight years of learning twenty of lessons

1. 100 individuals can take hard drugs and binge drink on a regular basis for an extended period of time without experiencing deep, dark longing or emptiness. One in 200 individuals will not be negatively affected. After many years of pondering this, I have concluded that Keith Richards is the exception, not the norm. He should be admired but cautiously imitated.

2. One in 300 individuals can have sex with three different strangers per week without frantically avoiding something. It could be their thoughts, pleasure, or body; it could be loneliness, love, growing old, or death. After many years of pondering this, I have concluded that Rod Stewart is the exception, not the norm. He should be admired but cautiously imitated.

3. The lyrics of the Smiths' 'Heaven Knows I'm Miserable Now' is the most neatly worded explanation of the reality of life and summarizes the initial optimism then collapsing bathos that is the first five years of one's twenties with elegant concision.

4. Life is difficult, difficult, sorrowful, unreasonable, and irrational. It makes so little sense. A great deal of it is unjust. And much of it boils down to the unsatisfying formula of good fortune and poor fortune.

5. Life is a wondrous, hypnotizing, magical, amusing, foolish entity. And humans are remarkable. We are all aware that we will perish, yet we continue to live. We exclaim and curse and care when the full bin bag breaks, yet with every minute that passes we edge closer to the end. We marvel at a nectarine sunset over the M25, the scent of a baby's cranium, and the efficiency of flat-pack furniture, despite knowing that everyone we love will one day cease to exist. I have no idea how we do it.

6. You are the sum total of everything that has happened to you up until the last sip of tea you just drained from your cup. The way your

parents hugged you and what your first suitor said about your thighs are all bricks that have been laid from the bottom up. Your eccentricities, foibles, and blunders are the result of things you've seen on television, things your instructors have said to you, and the way people have viewed you from the moment you first opened your eyes. Being a detective for your past, with the assistance of a professional, and tracing it all back to its origin, can be immensely beneficial and liberating.

7. However, therapy can only go so far. It's similar to the theory examination taken by new drivers. You can plan as much as you want on paper, but eventually you'll have to get in the car and fucking feel how everything functions.

8. Not everyone requires therapy to traverse their interiors. On some level, everyone is dysfunctional, but many individuals can function dysfunctionally.

9. Nobody is ever required to be in a relationship they do not want. openly   desire.

10. A vacation is entirely ruined if two cans of Boots insect repellent are not purchased at the airport on the way there. You'll never buy it when you get to the other end, and you'll spend every outdoor dinner with your traveling companions exclaiming, "I'm being eaten alive!" You speak passive-aggressively to one another because you're all irritated that someone forgot to bring it. Simply purchase it at the airport on your way out, and you're all set.
11. Do not consume sugar daily. Sugar is detrimental to your health both inside and out. Everything runs smoothly with three liters of water. A red wine chalice is medicinal.

12. No one has ever requested that you create for their birthday a floor-to-ceiling friendship collage. Or, contact them three times daily. No one will be upset if you don't invite them to dinner due to a lack of chairs. If you're fatigued by people, it's because you're playing the martyr to gain their favor. The issue is yours, not theirs.

13. It is futile and exhausting to attempt to make all of your decisions reflect your moral compass and then punish yourself when this plan invariably fails. Feminists can undergo waxing. Priests may profane. Vegans can sport leather footwear. As much good as possible. The substantial depiction of the world cannot depend on every choice you make.

4. Everyone ought to possess a Paul Simon album, a William Boyd book, and a Wes Anderson film. If these are the only three items on your rack, you can survive the longest, coldest, most lonely night.

15. If you are renting an apartment, paint the walls white, not ivory. Low-cost cream is filthy, suburban, and tacky. The color of cheap brilliant white is pure and calming.

16. When you select Shift and F3, the text becomes either all capital letters or all lowercase.

17. Allow others to snicker at you. Allow yourself to be vain. Mispronounce words. Yogurt is all over your clothing. The greatest relief comes from ultimately letting it happen.

18. You presumably don't have a wheat intolerance; you're simply not consuming enough wheat: 90–100g of pasta or two slices of bread. Everyone feels strange after consuming an entire pack of Hovis; similarly, you would feel strange after consuming an entire cantaloupe.

19. There is no faster way to unite a group of women than by bringing up the topic of coarse, stray facial hairs.

20. Sexual performance improves with age. If it continues to improve as it has thus far, I will be in a state of constant coitus at the age of ninety. There is no purpose in performing any additional actions. Possibly halting in the afternoon to consume a Bakewell slice.

21. It is perfectly acceptable to concentrate on yourself. You are permitted to travel, live independently, spend all your money on yourself, cavort with whomever you choose, and be as devoted to

your work as you wish. You are not required to marry or produce offspring. It is not a sign of shallowness to be unwilling to share your existence with a partner. However, it is completely unacceptable to be in a relationship if you want to be single.

22. Regardless of gender, age, or size, everyone looks great in a white shirt, thick polo neck, brown leather boots, denim jacket, or navy pea coat.

23. Try to remain on decent terms with your neighbors regardless of how awful they may be. Or make an ally with at least one occupant of the apartment next door with whom you can nod politely by the trash cans. There will be gas leaks and break-ins and packages that need to be delivered when you're out and it will all be so much simpler if you've always got someone whose door you can knock on. Smile and endure it. And provide them with a secondary set of your keys.

24. Try to imagine there is no Wi-Fi on the tube. It is utter garbage regardless. Always carry a book with you.

25. If you're feeling extremely overwhelmed with everything, try this: clean your room, answer all your unanswered emails, listen to a podcast, have a bath, go to bed before eleven.

26. Whenever feasible, you should swim naked in the sea. Make an effort to do it. If you are driving somewhere near the coast and you scent the salty tang of the ocean, stop the vehicle, strip off your clothes, and run until you are thigh-deep in the icy ocean.

27. You will have to choose between gel nail manicures and performing guitar as a way of life. Women cannot have both.

27a. Besides Dolly Parton.

28. Things will transform more drastically than you can fathom. Things will turn out 300 miles further north than your highest expectations. People in good health die in supermarket lines. The man seated next to you on the bus could be your future partner. Your

high school mathematics teacher and rugby coach may now be known as Susan. Everything will undergo transition. And it could happen at any time of day.

CHAPTER 26
Return home

There is a great deal I do not understand about love. First and foremost, I don't know what a relationship feels like for longer than a couple of years. Occasionally, I hear married people refer to a 'phase' of their relationship that persisted longer than my longest-ever relationship. Evidently, this is prevalent. People have referred to the first ten years of a relationship as "the honeymoon phase." My honeymoon phases have rarely lasted longer than ten minutes. Some of my friends describe their relationship as if it were a third individual in their partnership; a living entity that mutates, evolves, and grows the longer they are together. An organism that evolves at the same rate as two humans who spend a lifetime together. I have no idea what it means to care for that third being. I do not know what true, long-term love looks or feels like on the inside. I also do not know what it is like to live with the person you love. I do not know what it is like to go house-hunting with a partner or to conspire against an estate agent in the bathroom stall. I don't know what it's like to sleepily navigate my way around someone in the bathroom every morning as we take turns brushing our teeth and using the shower. I don't know what it's like to know you'll never be able to leave and return home; that your home is next to you every morning and night.

In fact, I do not know what it is like to be in a true team with a partner, as I have never relied on a romantic relationship for support or slowed down to its pace. But I've been in love and I've lost love, I know what it's like to leave and be left. I hope the remainder will eventually follow. I have learned nearly everything I know about love through my long-term friendships with women. Especially those I've lived with at some point. I understand what it is like to know every minute detail about a person and luxuriate in that knowledge as if it were a subject of study. Regarding the females with whom I've constructed homes, I'm comparable to a woman who can anticipate her husband's order at every restaurant. I am aware that India does not consume tea, that AJ's favorite sandwich is cheese and celery, that pastry gives Belle heartburn, and that Farly prefers her toast cold so that the butter spreads but does not melt. AJ requires eight hours of sleep to function, Farly requires seven, Belle requires around six, and India can get by on a Thatcherite four or five. Farly's alarm clock is Carole King's "So Far Away," and she enjoys viewing narrative-driven programs about obesity with titles such as Half-Ton Mom and My Son, The Killer Whale. Amazingly, AJ views old Home and Away episodes on YouTube and purchases books of sudoku to complete in bed. Before going to work, Belle watches exercise videos in her boudoir and bathes while listening to trance music. Every weekend, India does jigsaw puzzles in her chamber and watches Fawlty Towers. ('I just don't know how she gets the amusement out of it,' Belle once privately commented to me. There are twelve episodes total.)

I understand what it's like to enthusiastically don an oxygen tank and dive deep into a person's eccentricities and flaws, savoring every moment of intriguing discovery. For as long as I've known Farly, she has always slept in a gown. Why does she act this way? What is its purpose? Or, the fact that Belle rips off her flesh-colored tights on Friday evenings when she returns home from the office – is this a sign of her quiet rage against the corporate system, or merely a habit she has grown enamored of? AJ wraps a scarf around her cranium when she's exhausted; this is not cultural appropriation, however. Was she excessively swaddled as an infant, and does this give her a sense of infantilization? India enjoys sleeping with her comfort blanket, a frayed old navy sweater she names Nigh Nigh. Why does she refer to it as 'he'? And at what age did she determine it was a boy? In fact, I would love nothing more than to host a literary salon where all of my closest friends bring their childhood security blankets and we discuss the gender identities of each of them. Believe it or not, I would find that extremely persuasive.

I am familiar with collaboratively establishing and maintaining a residence. I am familiar with the concept of a shared economy based on trust; to know that there will always be someone willing to lend you £50 until payday, and that as soon as you pay it back, they may need to borrow the same amount from you (as Belle once described our salaries, "We're like elementary school children constantly swapping sandwiches"). 'One week you need my tuna and sweetcorn, the next I want your egg and cress'). I am familiar with the joy of receiving Christmas mail and greeting cards with three names on the front that make you feel like a family. When logging into online banking, I am familiar with the eerie sense of security induced by seeing three surnames on one account.

I understand how it feels to have an identity that is larger than yourself; to be part of a "us." I understand what it's like to overhear Farly saying, "We don't really eat red meat," or Lauren saying, "That's our favorite Van Morrison album," while conversing with a boy at a party. I understand how pleasantly surprising that feels. I am familiar with the process of transforming a negative experience into a shared mythology. We narrate our own micro-disasters in a similar manner to the couple whose luggage was misplaced during their most recent vacation, each taking a line. Like the time India, Belle, and I relocated and everything that could have gone awry did. The truth was lost keys, borrowing money from acquaintances, sleeping on sofas, and storing belongings. The narrative is excellent.

I understand what it is like to love someone and accept that you cannot alter certain characteristics about them; Lauren is a grammar snob, Belle is messy, Sabrina's texts are nonstop, AJ will never respond to me, and Fairly will always be moody when tired or hungry. And I know how liberating it is to be loved and accepted with all my faults (I'm always late, my phone is never charged, I'm oversensitive, I obsess over things, and I let the trash overflow) in return. I understand what it's like to listen to someone you care about regale a captive audience with a tale you've heard approximately five thousand times. I understand what it's like for that person (Lauren) to embellish it more flamboyantly each time, like an anecdotal Fabergé egg ('it occurred at eleven' becomes so this was around four a.m.'; 'I was seated on a plastic chair' becomes 'and I'm on this sort of chaise longue handcrafted from glass'). I understand what it's like to love someone so much that this doesn't bother you at all; to let them sing this well-rehearsed tune and perhaps even provide a supportive high-hat when they need to speed up the story. I am familiar with the feeling of a relationship in crisis. When you think: we either confront this thing and attempt to fix it or we go our separate ways. People only meet on the South Bank to reconcile or break up – I've done some of my best breaking up and breaking up in the National Theatre bar. I understand what it's like to feel as though you always have a lighthouse – lighthouses – to guide you back to dry land; to feel the warmth of its beam as it squeezes your hand at the interment of a loved one. Or to follow its light across a crowded room at a terrible party where your ex-boyfriend and his new wife have made an unannounced appearance; the flash that says Let's get chips and the night bus home.

I am aware that love can be boisterous and joyful. It could be dancing in the muck and rain at a festival while yelling "YOU ARE FUCKING AMAZING!" over the band. It is introducing them to your coworkers at a work event and beaming with pride as they make everyone giggle and make you appear lovable simply by virtue of their affection for you. It is chuckling until you cough. It is waking up in a foreign country that neither of you has visited before. At dawn, there is naked swimming. It is strolling down the street with someone on a Saturday night and feeling as though the entire city is yours. It is a large, gorgeous, vivacious natural force.

I am also aware that love is a relatively private phenomenon. It consists of lying on the sofa together while drinking coffee and discussing where you will go the following morning to consume more coffee. It involves folding the pages of books that you believe they will find intriguing. It's hanging up their laundry when they exit the house having moronically forgotten to take it out of the washing machine. As they hyperventilate on an easyJet flight to Dublin, the sign reads, "You're safer here than in a car; you're more likely to die in one of your Fitness First Body Pump classes than in the next hour." It consists of the following texts: "Hope today goes well," "How did today go?", "Thinking of you today," and "Picked up toilet paper." I am aware that love can occur under the splendor of the moon, stars, fireworks, and sunsets, but it can also occur while lying on blow-up air beds in a childhood bedroom, waiting in A&E or in line for a passport, or stuck in gridlock. Love is a calm, reassuring, relaxing, pedantic, harmonious hum; something you can easily forget is there, despite the fact that its arms are outstretched beneath you in case you collapse. Before it ended, I had lived with my companions for five years. First Farly left me for her fiancé, then AJ left, and finally India called me one day to tell me she was ready to leave as well, before bursting into tears.

I realized that an opportunity had been presented to me. I could wait until each of my acquaintances had found a partner and moved out on their own. I could rent from Gumtree strangers who kept shaving cream in the refrigerator in the expectation that I would soon find a man and leave. Alternatively, I could create a story on my own. Finding an affordable one-bedroom apartment to rent was difficult; I was shown a number of locations with beds next to the ovens and showerheads balanced over the toilet in a "wet room." There was the spacious one-bedroom' apartment that was twenty square meters in size, as well as the apartment with police tape around the front entrance. India accompanied me to viewings, negotiating and interrogating estate agents, and asking me if I truly believed I could live without a wardrobe and instead keep all my clothing in a suitcase under the bed.

Eventually, however, I was able to find a modestly priced apartment in the heart of Camden. It was a ground-floor apartment with a bedroom, toilet, and living room, closet space, and a shower that hung over a bathtub. Back of the house was a damp, sunken kitchen with no drawers that was so small I could scarcely turn around in it. The porthole window and canal view made me feel as though I were on a boat. It was not flawless, but it was mine. All of us who had lived together had a 'farewell flat-sharing' pub tour in our twenty-something haunts. We came costumed as an element of flat-sharing in our twenties, which was just as deranged as it sounds. AJ arrived as Gordon, our first landlord, replete with a leather biker jacket, white sneakers, a short brown wig, and a permanent smug grin. Farly, as the resident obsessive cleaner, appeared as a gigantic Henry vacuum in a spherical costume with an attached pipe that dragged along the ground the more she drank. With smudged lipstick and a Cher wig, Belle appeared as a boisterous nightmare neighbor. India appeared as a gigantic trash can, as emptying, relining, or removing one seemed to be the recurring motif of our time together, with bin liners tied around her shoes, a lid for a hat, and empty face-wipe and Monster Munch packets stuck to her body. People thought I was a

Marlboro Lights promotional girl pounding the sidewalks of Kentish Town and kept asking me for free cigarettes.

We went from pub to pub before returning to our original yellow-brick residence. We even visited Ivan at the corner store, only to learn from his coworker that he had inexplicably "gone abroad on unfinished business" and disappeared "without a trace."

Belle murmured wistfully, "The artists have left," as we walked along the crescent as day turned to twilight. Now the financiers will relocate. A week later, I placed my houseplants and books in cardboard crates and taped them up in preparation for my move. On our last night living together, India, Belle, and I consumed discounted Prosecco, the drink of the decade, and danced around our empty living room while listening to Paul Simon. The following morning, as we awaited our respective moving vehicles, we huddled in the corner of our wine-stained carpet, knees knocking together as we sat side by side and said very little.

The day I moved into my new apartment, Farley, the most efficient and organized person I will ever meet, assisted me with unpacking ('Are you sure you want to do this?'). I messaged her. She replied, "Please, this is like cocaine to me." We ordered Vietnamese cuisine and sat on my living-room floor slurping pho and dipping summer rolls in sriracha sauce as we discussed where to place the sofa, chairs, lamps, and shelves, as well as where I would write every day. We unpacked late into the evening before collapsing on my mattress against the bedroom wall, surrounded by cardboard crates of shoes, bags of clothing, and stacks of books. Farly had already departed for work when I awoke, and there was a note scrawled in her rotund, childlike handwriting, which hadn't changed since she wrote notes on my lever-arch files in Tipp-Ex during my science GCSE classes. It read, "I love your new home and I love you."

My mattress was covered in a vibrant white puddle caused by the morning sun seeping into my room. I stretched diagonally across the cool linen in my bed. I was entirely alone, but I felt safer than ever before. Not the bricks I somehow managed to rent or the roof over my head were the things I was most appreciative for. It was my house that I was carrying on my back like a tortoise. The feeling that

I was finally in caring and responsible hands. There was love in my vacant bed. It was stacked in the records that Lauren purchased for me when we were adolescents. It was on the soiled recipe cards from my mother that were tucked between the cookbook pages in my kitchen cabin. Love was in the bottle of gin tied with a ribbon that India had given me as a parting gift, and in the smudged photo strips with curled corners that would stick to my refrigerator. It was in the note that lay on the pillow next to me, the one I would fold and place in the shoebox with the other notes she had previously written. I awoke secure in my one-person canoe. I was floating in a sea of affection as I glided toward a new horizon. There it stood. Who would have known? It had always been there.

CHAPTER 27
Everything I Know at Age 28 About Love

A woman who is at ease with herself is preferable to one who performs tricks to impress a man. You should never have to exert effort to maintain a man's interest. If a man needs to be 'kept interested' in you, he has issues that are not your responsibility to manage.

You are unlikely to be best friends with the boyfriend of your closest friend. Give up that dream and bid goodbye to that fantasy. So long as he makes your friend pleased and you can tolerate his company during a lengthy lunch, everything will be fine.

Men enjoy nude women. All other frills and whistles are costly time-wasters.

Dating online is for the courageous. Those who take matters into their own hands – who pay a monthly fee for the opportunity to get closer to love, who fill out an embarrassing profile saying they're looking for a special someone to hold hands with in the supermarket – are romantic heroes of the highest order.

If you want a Brazilian wax, you should purchase one. If you don't want to, don't. If you enjoy feeling hairless and have the means to do so, wax year-round. Never purchase one for a man. And don't ever not get one for 'the sisterhood' – the sisterhood doesn't give a crap. Volunteer at a women's shelter instead of debating the politics of your pubic hair if you want to be useful. And never get one because you believe that not having one is filthy or unattractive; if that were the case, every unwaxed man alive would be unclean. (If possible, avoid hair-removal products at all costs.)

In the first few years following the end of a relationship, you may not be able to listen to the tracks of previous partners, but eventually those albums will find their way back to you. All of those memories of Saturdays by the sea and Sunday-night spaghetti on the couch will gently unfurl from the chords and rise, floating out of the songs until they vanish. There will always be a faint recognition that this song, or that man, was the center of your universe for a week, but at some point it will no longer make your pulse race.

If you continue to get inebriated and flirt with other people in front of your boyfriend, there is a problem in your relationship. Or, more likely, in your case. Explain why you require this level of attention immediately. Because no man on earth possesses sufficient immediate gratification to fill the void you feel.

The majority of the time, the affection you receive will be a reflection of the love you give yourself. If you cannot treat yourself with compassion, care, and patience, it is likely that no one else will.

How thin or fat you are has no bearing on the amount of affection you will receive or deserve.

With age, breakups become increasingly difficult. When one is young, a partner is lost. As you age, you lose a portion of your existence.

No practical consideration is sufficient to keep you in an unhealthy relationship. Vacations and weddings can be canceled, and residences can be sold. Do not conceal your timidity with pragmatic concerns.
If you lose regard for someone, you cannot fall in love with them again.

Integration into each other's lives should be equal; you should both make an effort to be involved with your friends, families, and careers. If it is unbalanced, you will experience resentment.

You should engage in sexual activity on the first date if it feels appropriate. You should never heed the counsel of a snarky self-help school of thought that portrays men as oxen and you as carrots. You are not a prize to be won; you are a human made of flesh, blood, entrails, and emotions. Sex is a consensual, respectful, joyous, creative, and collaborative experience, not a game of power.

There is no worse sensation than ending a relationship. At some point, the agony of being dumped can be converted into a new source of energy. The guilt and sorrow of breaking up with someone goes nowhere but inside you and, if you let it, will do circuits of your mind for eternity. I agree with Auden: "If equal affection cannot be, let me be the more loving."

There are numerous reasons why a person may be solitary at thirty, forty, or even one hundred and forty, none of which render them ineligible. Everyone has a past. Take the time to hear their perspectives.

Staying in someone's apartment – in their bed sheets, in their bedroom, or having them stay in yours – is even stranger than having sex with a complete stranger.

It is not anyone's responsibility to ensure your contentment. I'm sorry.

The ideal male is kind, humorous, and generous. He bends down to greet canines and then raises shelves. Looking like a tall Jewish pirate with the eyes of Clive Owen and the musculature of David Gandy should be a bonus, not a prerequisite.

Anyone is capable of being fucked. It is far superior to love than to be adored.

Do not imitate climax. It does absolutely no benefit for anyone. He is more than capable of dealing with the truth.

Casual intercourse can be very enjoyable if it's done for the right reasons and both parties are aware of the nature of the encounter. If you use it like an over-the-counter medication to feel better about yourself, the experience will be dreadfully disappointing.

The most thrilling part of a relationship is the first three months, when you are unsure if the other person will become your partner. The wonderful moment that follows is when you realize that person is yours. The portion that follows a few years later is something I have never encountered. According to reports, it's not always the most exciting, but I've heard it's the finest.

Unless someone dies, if a relationship goes wrong, you somehow had a role to play in it. How simultaneously liberating and daunting it is to realize this. Women are not better than males. Humans are humans, and we all make, permit, and facilitate errors.

The objective is intimacy; sloth is not.

Allow your peers to leave you once for a relationship. The excellent will always return.

On evenings when sleep feels impossible, you can lower your heart rate and drift off by daydreaming about the adventures you have yet to experience and the distances you've already traveled. Wrap your arms securely around your body, and as you do so, keep this thought in mind: I've got you.

Made in United States
North Haven, CT
11 August 2024